A Candlelight Ecstasy Romance ®

"WHERE DO YOU THINK I BELONG, HOME BAKING COOKIES FOR TWO KIDS AND A DOMINEERING HUSBAND?"

"No, Lindee, not in some man's kitchen. I see you pampered and loved in some man's bed."

"Look. I'm not at all interested in the way this conversation's going," she stated flatly, hoping her eyes wouldn't give away her true thoughts.

"I didn't figure you would be. But I know what's right," he murmured. "We're right, you and I."

"We can't, Brooks. Don't you see that no matter how I feel, I can't take the chance of being seen as some footloose woman having affairs with the men she meets along the campaign trail?"

Mockingly he taunted her, letting his words fall around her like a seductive cocoon. "Affairs? I was merely going to kiss you." Then he laughed, a quiet but hearty laugh, caught up in his own sense of pleasure. "Don't worry. Nobody's going to know a thing."

A CANDLELIGHT ECSTASY ROMANCE ®

KISS AND TELL

Paula Hamilton

A CANDLELIGHT ECSTASY ROMANCE ®

Published by
Dell Publishing Co., Inc.
1 Dag Hammarskjold Plaza
New York, New York 10017

Dell ® TM 681510, Dell Publishing Co., Inc.
Candlelight Ecstasy Romance®, 1,203,540, is a registered
trademark of Dell Publishing Co., Inc., New York, New
York.

ISBN: 0–440–14542–2

Printed in the United States of America
First printing—April 1984

*This book is dedicated
to Tommy and to Lydia,
the Believers*

To Our Readers:

We have been delighted with your enthusiastic response to Candlelight Ecstasy Romances®, and we thank you for the interest you have shown in this exciting series.

In the upcoming months we will continue to present the distinctive sensuous love stories you have come to expect only from Ecstasy. We look forward to bringing you many more books from your favorite authors and also the very finest work from new authors of contemporary romantic fiction.

As always, we are striving to present the unique, absorbing love stories that you enjoy most—books that are more than ordinary romance.

Your suggestions and comments are always welcome. Please write to us at the address below.

Sincerely,

The Editors
Candlelight Romances
1 Dag Hammarskjold Plaza
New York, New York 10017

CHAPTER ONE

"Ladies and gentlemen, my dear friends, I hope you will join your fellow Texans in supporting . . ." For the briefest instant Lindee Bradley stopped her speech. It was simply too unbelievable. At first she'd only caught a glimpse of the top part of his head—faint gold strands of light shimmering in contrast to thick dark waves of hair—but then she'd looked once more, a little closer this time. The well-known television newscaster who was supposed to be capturing her words for the six o'clock news was yawning. Not any ordinary quiet yawn, but rather a noisy, gaping one that was attracting far more of the audience's attention right now than were her words.

Assuming a jaunty pose, he stood along the edge of the crowd of people, beaming a smile that exuded a self-possessed air. That the tall, attractive man knew he was on top of things showed in his every nuance. And what disturbed Lindee Bradley the most was that it didn't bother him one damned bit that he'd interrupted her speech, destroyed her train of thought, and distracted everyone in the audience so that they weren't listening to what she had to say. And it certainly wasn't the first time. In the five days he'd been around he'd managed to turn everything topsy-turvy.

All the hours of preparation and planning to make this speech before the Texas Cattlemen's Association successful could be destroyed by this cocky reporter who cared not one whit about her campaign but was obviously reveling in the attentions of the crowd. She stifled a gasp when she saw that he had begun nodding and speaking to some of the people standing near him.

Loudly she cleared her throat. Regaining her composure she went on. ". . . in supporting my bid to become the new senator from District Twenty-seven who'll serve all the people of this great state. I'll do everything in my power to make you proud."

The applause that followed made her smile. Despite three months of heavy campaigning Lindee still felt a warmth, an undefinable glow, each time a group of people applauded her, and the fact that these individuals weren't her constituents didn't bother her in the least. Each and every one of them were political and financial assets. And right now their applause helped her forget the inexcusable behavior of Brooks Griffin, Texas's answer to Dan Rather and the most insolent man she'd ever met.

Looking down along the first row of people in the Fort Worth hotel ballroom, Lindee caught her mother's eye. Without words they mutually agreed that her speech had been just right for this audience. Nothing too strong; an upbeat message of the state's economic future. The people in this room were some of the most influential representatives of ranchers and cattlemen of Texas. They could offer big money and big contributions, and Lindee knew she needed both right now to see her campaign for state senator through to the November election fifteen days away.

Suddenly she lost her train of thought when Brooks Griffin drew her gaze from across the room. He eyed her speculatively for a second and then gave her a knowing grin that stirred her emotions. He was all too sure of himself.

Brooks stood back from the crowd, aware that he'd caught her eye. Briefly he let himself wonder what Lindee Bradley must think about him. Then he sent her a mocking grin, telling himself that whatever she thought probably wouldn't be good. She didn't like him much. He could feel the tension in her whenever he went

12

near her, and when he'd tried to talk to her she'd given him a cold shoulder that he swore could make icicles appear.

But it really didn't matter at this point. He'd already made up his mind about her, and he wasn't a man to be denied. From the first time he'd met her, he'd known he had to have her. She was an enigma—bright, attractive, totally in control one moment, and then changing to hellacious fireworks the next—and he was immensely curious about her. Lindee Bradley was too much of a woman for him to let pass by.

Lindee looked away and then glanced back in surprise. He'd started out of the room, headed for the area where the press was scheduled to interview her later. But before he closed the door behind him he looked at her and cast a quick conspiratorial wink her way. Thinking maybe she was mistaken, she stared at him for another moment, just long enough to see him do it again. A seething rage gripped her once again. Of all the damned nerve!

Gathering up the sheets that contained her neatly typed speech, she told herself she had to forget him as she straightened a stray lock of hair that fell along her brow. She had to concentrate on her campaign instead.

By this time she'd given up trying to count how many hotel meeting rooms she'd been in, how many bland cold meals she'd eaten, or how many handshakes she'd shared. After a while every place looked the same and every meal tasted just like the one before. But tonight was different. She was standing in one of the finest hotels in Fort Worth, Texas, inside a room that blatantly exuded luxury from its magnificent imported crystal chandeliers to its Oriental carpeting. And Lindee was willing to bet that within this very ballroom stood a group of Texans whose total wealth could be in the billions. It was a heady feeling, she had to admit, and everything had gone fairly smoothly until recently.

With a will as strong as steel and a fierce sense of independence to match, Lindee had jumped into this senate race without telling a soul. For a long time she'd known this was precisely what she wanted, and yet the pressure and demands on her were great.

13

Not only had sleep become a valued luxury with her hectic schedules that never seemed to stop, but there was also the continual need for handshaking and telegraphic conversation, fueled by the unrelenting attentions from the media and her public.

Yet the real thorn in her side was proving to be Brooks Griffin. A highly respected television newscaster who'd been assigned by WBCX in Houston, the largest television station in the state of Texas, to cover her campaign, he'd managed to unnerve her and send her emotions reeling. What he'd done tonight was just one in what seemed to be a never-ending series of episodes that had occurred since his arrival five days ago.

Firmly she shrugged the intrusive newsman out of her thoughts once again. A slow-breaking smile spread across her face when with long graceful fingers she lifted her rich chestnut hair off her neck and absentmindedly let it fall down along her shoulders. There was a buzz throughout the room as people broke their polite silences and began talking.

Lindee watched her mother, Vivian Bradley, widow of the late state senator Max Bradley and veteran campaigner, as she stood up and immediately began shaking the hands of those around her. At the age of sixty-three her mother was intent upon one thing: helping her daughter win a seat in the state senate. Nobody on her campaign staff had proven to be the kind of trouper Vivian Bradley was. She had the energy of a young colt, making her daughter feel a little guilty at times for not always loving everything about their lives right now.

Lindee left the podium and went through the side door, readying herself mentally for the photo session with the reporters. She'd leave her mother to visit with the important people who'd attended. Vivian was a master at the subtleties of raising funds.

The anteroom was empty, and Lindee started to turn back, thinking she'd stepped through the wrong door. A deep voice stopped her.

"Don't go. The others will be here in a minute." Brooks Griffin leaned against one of the tall windows that framed one

14

side of the room, the lights from the street illuminating his commanding silhouette.

"Mr. Griffin," she said, walking purposefully toward him. She didn't stop until she was standing face-to-face with him, staring directly at this arrogant man.

A smile crossed his face. "Yes, Miss Bradley?"

Shaking inside, she kept her voice low and deceptively smooth. "What you did out there is not to happen again. I didn't appreciate it one damned bit."

He moved away from the window, closing off the distance between them. For the very first time she studied him intensely, noticing the piercing darkness of his guarded brown eyes, the smooth fullness of his cheeks, and the well-defined cut of his jaw. No wonder so many women were drawn to him for his good looks. The television cameras didn't do him justice.

His voice broke through her thoughts. "I'm not sure I know what you're talking about."

Catching the gleam in his eye, she knew he was laughing at her. Stopping only long enough to square her shoulders, she took him on. "Don't be ridiculous, Mr. Griffin, you know very well what I'm referring to . . . your purposefully distracting my audience the way you did," she said tersely, trying to restrain her rage long enough to tell him precisely what she thought.

Impulsively, his smile broke into a wide grin, making that abrasive, challenging part of him momentarily fade away, but then he answered her. "A politician's supposed to get along with the media. Hasn't your campaign manager told you that yet?"

Unwilling to hear another word from his lips, Lindee raised her hand to stop him. "Mr. Griffin, I'm issuing you fair warning right now. If you ever pull another stunt like this again, I'll have you off this tour before you can pack your dirty shirts." Filled with a new sense of calm, she stared directly at the man who was so intent upon making her life unpleasant. She hadn't known what she was going to say until she'd spoken, but she didn't regret it at all.

"Hey, wait a minute, lady. Just hold on. I don't work for you so I don't have to jump when you crack the whip." His eyes burned through her. "And while we're at it, I'll tell you this." His face softened as his humor returned. "If I did work for you I'd see that your speeches had just a touch more drama to them. If you're trying to drum up financial contributions, you're going to have to be a little more aggressive when you make a speech. Those people out there are tough. They still have one boot back in the old days when women were taken care of, not running state politics. Besides all that, I couldn't help my yawning. Yawning is an involuntary response, you know."

Her surprise made her hesitate. How dare this brash man say that to her? He acted as though she were boring, and she felt her anger turn to fury. "I would think you'd know how to conduct yourself in a more civilized manner, Mr. Griffin, and as for my speeches, if you don't like them you don't have to listen!"

All he did was laugh then, and that made things even worse. What would she have to do to convince him to take her seriously?

"You're a fiery thing, aren't you?" he said, staring at her. "You're beautiful when you're angry. Something about that anger of yours gives off just the right spark in those hazel eyes," he managed between laughs. "Maybe you should show more of this side of your personality to the voters. It might help."

"Why don't you just pack up all your political advice and . . . and give it to a candidate who's interested," she fumed, thinking of other things she wanted to say, but trying not to demean herself.

"Sorry, Miss Bradley, but I'm here to do my job. I don't always get to pick my assignments."

"That's surprising," she countered coldly. "The way you act I thought perhaps you owned WBCX." Her fury was mounting with every arrogant word he spoke. She could feel her pulse race wildly as her body responded to what seemed to be imminent danger. "Anything else? Do you want to tell me anything more I need to know? I'm sure my campaign manager will be happy to hear that you've analyzed my approach, found it lacking, and

16

have advised me of what I should do next." She took a deep breath before going on. It was important that she put this man in his place now, before she was forced to do so publicly.

"My next piece of advice is this," he interrupted, never bothering to conceal his self-satisfied smile. "Don't be so resistant to suggestions. You never know what you might learn if you let yourself open up—be receptive . . . and a little more reasonable."

Her mouth opened in astonishment, but she recovered, and in a voice that could cut through a diamond she answered, "Well, then, I'm sure you'd want me to show you just how reasonable I am. I think it best for you to leave my campaign. I think that's reasonable." What could he possibly do but agree?

Admiring her quick thinking, he eyed her speculatively for a moment. "Oh, I don't know. Now that I think about it, this assignment's getting better by the minute, and I haven't finished with what I want to do just yet. Why don't you and I have a drink after this and talk it over?"

She was seeing red. "Talk it over? Are you kidding? I have nothing to say to you. Nothing!"

"On the contrary, you've talked almost nonstop since you came in here," he argued. "You're very articulate, you know."

A storm of emotions swept through her. She couldn't stand his overconfident, strong bearing, or the obvious way he had of twisting her words until they held very different meanings, yet she wouldn't lie to herself. There was something about him that was intriguing, almost compelling, and her entire body reacted to it. "I can see that this conversation is going nowhere."

"Why don't we take it somewhere—the two of us? We can go to your room or mine," he said in a persuasive voice. "I find you more exciting by the minute, Lindee. It's okay for me to call you Lindee, isn't it?"

Coldly she replied, "I'd prefer that you not call me that. Somehow you make it sound a little too personal. Miss Bradley sounds better coming from you."

Undaunted, he went on. "That crazy about me, huh? Well, I could tell you weren't able to resist my subtle charm."

"The only charm you have is . . . oh, never mind. Why don't you just stay away—from me and my campaign," she snapped. "Find yourself a candidate who'll be more amusing."

A door opened behind them and the reporters swarmed into the room, effectively ending their conversation as Lindee stormed away.

Brooks's voice cut across to her one last time. "I didn't say you weren't amusing, Lindee." His voice played with her name. "On the contrary, I find you highly amusing. . . ."

She didn't bother to answer, but she told herself as she moved to the center of the room that the man had to be stopped. His blind ambition had gotten him here; now it was up to her to get rid of him. He might need the headlines, but she didn't need the irritation.

Hurriedly, but with an efficiency that was ample demonstration of their professionalism, the reporters gathered around Lindee, measuring the distance from her face to their microphones and cameras before asking the first question, making certain that they caught the candidate's words. The noise died down when Lindee began to speak.

Brooks had planned his questions carefully, hoping to challenge her views on land conservation. It would be an appropriate subject to bring up after she had addressed the biggest landowners in Texas. He stepped to the side, posing for his cameraman.

"Miss Bradley," he said, and then nothing. The well-prepared question stuck in his throat the instant she turned to face him, stirring to life a wealth of emotions that caught him off guard. Dammit, what was going on with him? Why was he all of a sudden playing the fool? He'd done this once before, on the day he met her. It wasn't like him to lose control. Something crazy was going on.

Lindee answered another reporter's question while Brooks worked to regain his composure. He noticed his cameraman looking at him with an air of surprise, but Brooks ignored him. What could he possibly say? What excuse could he give? That there was something special about this woman? That was ridiculous. But as soon as he thought it, he knew it wasn't ridiculous at all. There *was* something special about her, and he couldn't quite put his finger on it. She wasn't the most beautiful woman he'd ever come across, perhaps, but she had a certain appeal that had kept him distracted and slightly off target since he'd met her.

Twice he'd lost his cool, although he had always taken pride in his strong sense of professionalism. This wasn't like him, he knew, but then she wasn't anything like the candidate he'd expected to meet. He could have described every one of her assets if he had had the time, but he didn't. She was finished with the photo sessions and the questions from the press. He watched her walk over to her mother's side.

"Oh, Lindee, darling, you were wonderful, absolutely wonderful tonight," her mother enthused. "And you seemed so confident, darling." Dropping her voice down into a stage whisper, Vivian went on. "I think you're finally becoming more relaxed around those television cameras, dear."

Always a mother, Lindee thought to herself before saying what was uppermost in her mind. "If that man weren't always disturbing things, and in general trying to throw me off, I could do much better, believe me."

"Lindee, lower your voice," her mother begged. "Who on earth are you talking about?" Vivian's curiosity had got the best of her.

"Him," Lindee said, and then stared daggers in the direction of Brooks Griffin.

With one hand thrust deep in the pants pocket of his expensive gray suit and his angular chin held high, the too aggressive reporter stood only a few feet away, coolly appraising her. It seemed he spent a great deal of his time merely watching her, and she didn't like the feeling it gave her. The blood raced to her face when she thought of how much trouble he'd brought to her life at a time when she least needed it. Unable to prove it, she knew that Brooks Griffin would do anything to sabotage her chances of winning. Everything he had done since they first met had been directed against her, and she'd heard the rumor more than once that he supported her opponent.

Brooks Griffin had interrupted one of her press conferences with irrelevant news, then he'd virtually ignored her, except for his persistent staring, acting as if she were merely a token female contender. Then he'd teased and embarrassed her during a very important meeting the day before, and if that weren't enough, he'd already taken it upon himself to give her a lecture on getting ahead in the world of politics. At least she could take some comfort in knowing that the invincible Mr. Griffin hadn't been able to fire off one question during *this* press conference.

Nonetheless, she assured herself, she'd talk to Earl, her campaign manager, later. WBCX might be the most influential television station in the entire state, but they'd have to assign someone else to her. She'd had quite enough of Mr. Brooks Griffin.

Her mother watched her expression. "Now, Lindee, forget about him. You mustn't be too hasty in your judgment of people, darling. This man is an up-and-comer. Everyone says he's only a step away from national television, and everyone on your campaign staff seems to like him."

They both glanced over at him again, and from across the room Brooks sent them a smile so engaging that Lindee could well imagine why the women viewers of Texas were captivated by him. Besides his notoriety as a crack reporter, he obviously had the capacity to be a real charmer when he wanted. She'd seen his charm in action several times already, but it hadn't worked on her.

"He's going to be a real celebrity one day soon," her mother went on, but not before she'd returned his smile through the crush of people. "It's such a distinct honor for him to be here working side by side with you on your campaign. It wouldn't hurt you to be nicer to him."

Lindee watched him. He hadn't taken his eyes off her for the last several minutes. When he saw her look his way he winked just as he'd done before, as if between them they shared some secret.

"Nicer?" Lindee turned her back to him, feeling her cheeks redden with the animosity she felt. "Are you kidding? I'm going to get rid of that man as soon as possible. Good night, Mother." She started to walk away.

"Lindee." Her mother reached out to stop her, her voice strained in a muffled whisper. "You know you've been honored by having this man assigned to your campaign. I can't help but think about his being the youngest man ever presented with the Golden Mike award a few years ago. Why, he's famous. In Texas, at least," she added. A deep frown twisted her attractive face, aging her as she spoke. "His being here can only mean, dear, that people think you have a chance of winning. Otherwise they'd never have considered sending him out to cover your campaign, not a man like Brooks Griffin. Now, please, just try to be nice. He's only been around a few days, and you have only fifteen more days to go. Try to think of it that way, dear."

Vivian took her daughter's hand in hers and held it close for a moment before walking out of the room with her. She alone knew the price that must be paid if her daughter were to be elected, and she planned to make sure that everything happened exactly as it should and that nothing, absolutely nothing, would stand in the way of her daughter's winning.

The elevator door opened and Lindee stepped out, searching for her keys in her evening bag. She'd said good night to her mother and now looked forward to getting some sleep. Finding her keys, she tucked her bag under her arm and walked slowly down the carpeted hallway, suddenly aware of the solemn silence of the vast empty space.

"Hello again," a voice boomed out from the shadows.

Quickly she turned. "What on earth do you want?" she gasped, trying to slow down her racing heart. She'd been a thousand miles away in her thoughts.

"I asked you earlier to meet me. You never gave me an answer." Brooks Griffin stepped out of the darkness. He knew now why she had this crazy power over him. He watched how her topaz eyes widened in surprise, and suddenly he knew.

She had everything—looks, brains, a sultry sensuality, a sense of her own destiny, and, he hoped, a touch of humor, although she'd done nothing to let him see it. Only her interactions with other people told him his hunch was probably correct.

She stopped and stared at him, amazed at how sure he was of himself. "Let's get serious! I had no intention of meeting you, and I certainly didn't give you any encouragement."

He grinned, and this time he looked like a mischievously handsome little boy. "I've met lots of women who like to play hard to get, Lindee. I don't mind playing your game . . . for a while, anyway." Casually he walked over to where she stood, not stopping until he was so close she could feel the heat of his body.

She backed away, momentarily caught off guard by his approach as well as by his words. He never took his eyes away from hers, but she couldn't read his expression. Brooks Griffin was undoubtedly proving to be the most exasperating man she'd ever met.

"Let's get one thing straight, shall we? I'm not playing any games with you, Mr. Griffin. First of all, that's not my style. In the second place, you're not the kind of man I'd be interested in." She stepped around him and proceeded down the hallway, intent upon reaching her room. She put her key in the door.

"Okay, okay," he called, doggedly following her. "We'll play it your way. No pun intended."

She looked at him then, almost allowing herself to smile at the distinct way he had of twisting and playing with words. "What do I have to do to make you understand me, Mr. Griffin?"

"Call me Brooks." He noticed the way her breasts strained against the silk dress as she took a deep breath and held it. He could feel the electricity that connected him to her.

"Look, let's just end this right here and now."

He didn't say anything. He merely stood looking at the way her eyes darkened when she was angry, remembering how her face lit up when she laughed. He'd studied her many times since his assignment to her campaign, but never quite this closely.

Wishing he'd do something—answer her—leave—anything—she went on, her frustration mounting. "I'm not interested in you and I really don't know why you'd be interested in me. Actually, Mr. Griffin, you and I don't even like each other. I know that you're supporting Ted Bullock for state senator. I've heard it from just about everyone."

His eyes made a quick assessing sweep of her, and he felt his blood run hot. "I think you're fascinating. I've never met a female politician of your stature—not one as young and attractive as you, anyway. Most of the women in politics who I know are either pushing retirement age or grandmothers or both."

"Your reputation precedes you, Mr. Griffin. And I suppose with your winking at me and your suggestive glances, I'm to consider your attentions flattering. Am I correct?" She lifted her gaze to his, intent upon defiance, only to be caught up by the fire that danced in his eyes.

"I'd like that."

"You have an incredible amount of nerve. Do you know that?"

"Thank you."

"I didn't intend that as a compliment."

"Well, I took it as one, regardless of your intent. And while we're at it, Lindee, I'm going to tell you something else—for your own good."

She held up her hand to him. She was shaking like a leaf. "I don't want to hear any more advice from you tonight. You've given me enough political enlightenment to last forever." Something told her she'd better end this conversation quickly. She felt more than a little disturbed by the way her pulse was racing.

"This doesn't happen to be about politics."

"Oh?"

"No, it's personal."

"Haven't I made it clear enough to you?" she charged, her voice filled with exasperation. "I'm not interested in your ideas

23

about my politics and I'm even less interested in your personal opinions about me. Now, good night!" Angrily she twisted the key and pushed open the door to her hotel room.

He reached out and wrapped his hand around her arm, stopping her. His voice rang out in a husky echo, somehow reminding her of dark nights and solitary sandy beaches.

"Just one thing more and then I'm through. Don't look at a man with those soulful eyes of yours again—not the way you looked at me earlier. If you do, you're going to have men standing at your bedroom door just like I am now. It's dangerous, that look of yours . . . and incredibly sexy."

His hand reached out to stroke the glowing sheen of her hair. He gave her a moment to resist and then let his fingers lightly touch the strands of hair that fell around her face. "You have beautiful hair." It was a sincere observation, made as though she weren't even there.

Shock rippled through her. Immediately she pulled away and stood against the door frame, wondering what it was about this man that made her think of life, of a mysterious kind of vitality that she hadn't known before. It was as if he held some secret knowledge—one she longed to know. But his touch was too unsettling. Somehow it had been deeply personal; too intimate.

Shaking her head, Lindee pushed all those ridiculous thoughts from her mind. Too many long hours, too little time for intimacy, had suddenly led her to this irrational, preposterous romanticizing with a man she detested.

"I think we've said enough for one night. Good evening, Mr. Griffin," she said. "I hope you and I won't be bothered by each other again." She closed the door behind her and breathed a deep sigh—of relief, of regret, of undefinable confusion—steeped with an interplay of sensations she'd kept bottled up for a very long time.

Later that night when the shadows of evening gave way to the curtain of darkness, she told herself to sleep. Totally exhausted, she tried to close her mind to everything around her, but discordant thoughts cluttered her consciousness and refused to let her rest. And so, as she so often did when there was nothing else to do but wait for body and mind to relax, she urged herself to let go of all her troubles and dream a fantasy. A little too quickly vivid images fluttered before her mind's eye, and when she recognized them for what they were she tried to push them aside, but like herself they were strong, and they refused to go.

Lindee and Brooks were standing together in a dark room, but she could see that there was a bed and a table and a chair. Everything was painted stark white, and the sheets floated across the bed as though a fan were blowing some steady breeze over it. Locked in an embrace, she and Brooks were whispering to each other; words she couldn't hear. Through the shadows she could see the strong angular lines of his face, softened by the magic of the night. Her own face was darkened, unclear, but she knew it was herself.

Then she saw him move and stand away from her for a moment, and in slow-motion gestures he began to undress, first unfastening his shirt from the neck to the upper edge of his belt. He stood there, said something, and reached for his belt buckle, released it, and with one further motion he began unbuttoning his pants. Lindee reached out and touched him then, and she could plainly see her own long, slender fingers trace idle lines through the curled hair on his chest. Practically able to feel it in reality, Lindee was caught up in the spell of her fantasy, feeling the suggestive pull as she became more and more relaxed.

He turned her toward a tiny sliver of light that came from somewhere out of view, and Lindee heard him say, "It's you I want. No others." And his voice was deep and husky, so mesmerizingly enticing that she strained to hear more, but nothing else was said. Now she could see that he was staring knowingly into her eyes, prolonging the mood of the moment.

Pulling her to him, he wrapped his arms around her and began to plant soft kisses all along her face, stopping only when he'd found her lips. She clung to him in steadfast wonder, absorbing all the fevered unfamiliar sensations of the man, and after a while

25

she saw herself reach up and weave her hands through the soft folds of his shirt until she was caressing the taut muscles of his back, kneading his flesh with her fingers, lost in the sheer magnetic power of this sensual man.

In aggressive abandon she pulled her hands away and reached for the lowest button of his shirt, catching his eyes with hers, having no use for words, her eyes saying it all. When at last he was standing naked before her she drank in the very sight of him. He was magnificent, strong, virile, and as silently suggestive as any man she'd ever dreamed of.

With warm hands he took off her dress and unhooked her bra, sliding the garments off her body with dreamlike ease. As he worked his hands to free her he was setting fire to her very being with his gentle kisses that left no part of her untouched by his lips.

Peering into the gauzelike haze of her dream, Lindee watched Brooks as he stood back, silently taking in the way she looked, never letting his dark eyes stray, as though he'd never really seen her before. He gazed at the light in her pale eyes, and then down at her small nose that peaked above the soft line of her curved lips. Her hair was down, full and long, filled with dancing red lights that changed with each subtle twist of her head.

Then she saw him study her body much as an artist might look at his model. She saw the interest that was awakened in his own body as he let his gaze run from the smooth calves of her legs, up over her firm hips and narrowed waist, to the very peaks of her breasts. She knew he approved of what he saw. His eyes told her as much.

And then it was her turn. Brooks was willing, seemingly wanting her to match his own interest. From the top of his head to the tips of his toes she studied him as thoroughly and completely as she'd ever examined anything. After all, it was her dream.

If she hadn't known he was a reporter she could well envision him as an athlete. His physique was that of a man in superb condition; she gazed at the broad shoulders, lean rib cage, and taut muscle tone that complemented his build. She longed to

26

touch the sleek and smoothly planed flesh of his thighs. It fascinated her that this man was mere flesh, but so strong, so unyieldingly masculine. An impulse so powerful she could not control it swept over her. She wanted to run her fingers through the coarse dark hairs of his chest, longed to kiss, to possess, this ghostly shadow.

Then he took her breasts one at a time into his mouth, awakening in her a sensation so overwhelming that she moved in her sleep, not quite believing it was a dream. When he began to run his hands up and down her body, working her to a feverish pitch, she reached out for him, and in unison they lay down on the ethereal bed, where they suddenly vanished into thin air.

Lindee awoke then and looked around the room, letting her eyes take in every dark corner, listening for any strange sound. *What are you doing?* her mind fairly shouted at her. *Fool, fool, fool.* She felt the words reverberate in her head. *How could you even begin to let yourself think about Brooks?*

Appalled by her dream, she berated herself. *Get yourself under control, and do it fast before you lose all your perspective as well as this campaign. You don't even like this man,* her mind insisted.

Restlessly tossing on the suddenly uncomfortable bed, she knew she didn't want romance right now. Anything but. Her dream had been just that—a dream of idle fantasy so far from real life that it could only be laughable.

Go to sleep, she admonished herself, trying her damnedest to deny the rich warm feeling that had engulfed her body as she dreamed. She jammed her head into her pillow. *Don't ever let yourself remember how warm and tender his hands had felt in that wildly ridiculous vision of yours.*

A ragged sigh escaped her lips. She didn't want to think about Brooks Griffin, and certainly not in the darkest hours of the night.

She would admit that there were times when she longed to find a man who could match her, ambition for ambition, ideal for ideal, dream for dream. But Lindee had set out to become a state senator, and she'd made a vow to let nothing stand in her way.

Her dream man would have to remain only a dream. Her life was dedicated to one cause and one cause only right now, and no man—especially a man like Brooks—was going to be able to distract her, consciously or subconsciously.

CHAPTER TWO

"I don't care how many yellow roses that man sends me, Earl. I'm not about to change my mind. Absolutely not." Lindee felt all the rage from the previous night wash over her again. The first thing she'd thought of when she'd opened her eyes had been her dream—that insane, bewildering fantasy—and here in the light of day reality seemed far, far different.

Now she sat curled up on the sofa in the living room of the hotel suite, still dressed in her robe, her mouth tasting like cotton, and her long hair fanning out along her shoulders in wild disarray. If she'd known everyone on the campaign staff was going to be in the suite when she woke up, she'd have dressed first, but all she'd wanted was coffee, and when she had stepped quietly out of her bedroom after calling room service, she'd walked in on a full-scale meeting. It took only one quick look at their troubled faces for her to know she was in for a fight.

After closing the door in Brooks Griffin's face last night she'd called the manager of WBCX and asked that he send another reporter to replace Mr. Griffin. And now, from the looks of things, every single person in the room was anxiously waiting his turn to let her know what a mistake she was making.

She had no illusions whatsoever about Brooks Griffin. She

didn't trust any man who had such overwhelming ambition, not when there was a chance that she could be used as the next stepping stone on his way to the top. Demanding, forceful, irritating, challenging—he was all of those things and more. He rubbed her the wrong way, kept her feeling uptight whenever he was around—watching her every move. Was he waiting for her to make a mistake? She felt as if that were precisely what he wanted. It was enough to drive her mad.

"Okay, let's hear it. We might as well clear the air." She looked across the sofa to her mother. "I didn't know you'd still be here. I thought you were leaving."

"I was, dear." Vivian nodded. "But I decided to catch a later flight back to San Antonio."

She listened as Earl Gillespie took the lead, watching the way he formed the sincere words, reminding herself that not only was he her campaign manager, but he was also her dearest friend, a man Lindee trusted implicitly.

"Lindee, it's just no good. It doesn't make much difference what you think about Brooks right now. You need him to be with you for the remaining days of the campaign." He sat to her right in a worn armchair, picking at the broken threads of the chair with an air of distraction, his expression as grave as her mother's. "I'm just asking you to think about it a little while longer. That's all. Don't be so quick to decide something so important to you."

As he finished speaking there was a knock on the door. Earl answered it, and after tipping the waiter, rolled the breakfast cart into the room.

Earl poured Lindee her first cup of coffee while the others sat quietly watching the drama being played out before them. They knew their turn could come soon.

"Mother, do you agree with Earl? Although I don't know why I bother to ask." Lindee looked straight at her.

"Lindee, Mr. Griffin can get you on national news. He thinks so, and so do we."

Sipping the hot coffee, she made herself count to ten, not

wanting to snap at her mother, yet full of disbelief. There was absolutely no way that she could believe what he'd done could have been good for her career. And yet she had to be honest with herself. She was just like all the others. She'd felt a certain awareness, an attraction to him right from the first. Magnetic—that was the only way to describe Brooks Griffin. Dangerous too.

Watching her mother nervously twist the lace edge of her handkerchief, Lindee felt tired all over again, as if she hadn't slept all night. Plainly she didn't need this hassle right now. None of them did.

"Mother, Brooks Griffin has been abrasive . . . almost contentious, since the first time he and I met. He doesn't even think I can win this damned election. He's supporting Bullock. All of you think he's so wonderful, such a benefit to this campaign. Well, I'm warning you." Her voice rose. "If I let him stay he's going to destroy it."

Like a little child she rubbed her eyes. So this was the way it was to be, she thought. Well, she couldn't go on like this. Even her normally high spirits were flagging now. There was an air of tension all around her.

She bit her lip. Why on earth was all this happening right now? It didn't seem fair. "Earl, tell me what's happening with Senator Bullock's women's rights bill. I heard Brooks's news commentary last night, and I was surprised." She was eager to get on with her business, to discuss issues, not people.

"I didn't have a chance to tell you. That was my mistake. Yesterday Bullock withdrew it from consideration—said he'd wait until after the election to bring it up again. The women voters are not going to be happy about that."

"That sounds strange. He's up to something, Earl." She thought for a moment. "The women voters would want to stick with him so that he'd get this bill through for them, right?"

"Probably. But it's plain to see that he'll use every trick in the book. Bullock's running scared."

"And Brooks Griffin must know it too," she said thoughtfully.

31

"Who sent the flowers? Brooks or WBCX?" she asked, stalling for time so that she could think.

"His name's on each of the cards. They started coming early this morning." Her mother smiled when she saw Lindee look around. There must have been four dozen of the pale yellow roses in assorted floral vases. The sweet aroma filled the room.

"Lindee," Earl's assistant Steve said as he got up to leave, "Brooks wants to interview you today. I told him I'd let him know by eleven o'clock. Think it over. If you decide to do the interview, I've set it up for one o'clock out on the balcony here. It's up to you."

"Thanks, Steve."

When he closed the door behind him no one said much. Everything had already been said; now it was up to her.

"I'm going to take a shower." She stood up and pulled her robe tightly around her. "I'll let you all know by eleven o'clock." She looked over at her mother. "Are you flying back home today?"

"Yes, dear." Her mother nodded. "I've got to get everything ready for when you come home. We'll have the biggest party San Antonio has ever seen." Her eyes twinkled, and Lindee knew she was already thinking about the busy schedule she had to look forward to. This campaigning was in her blood.

"Okay, Mother, I'll see you then. Thanks for everything." Lindee leaned down to kiss her mother's cheek, but Vivian motioned toward her bedroom and then followed her.

"One more thing, dear," she said when Lindee had closed the bedroom door. "I think you're on the verge of making a very big mistake. No matter what you think of him, Brooks is an asset, and you can't afford to cut yourself off from him. Besides all that, he's willing to apologize."

Lindee had to remind herself to be patient. Her mother only wanted what was best for her, and normally she didn't push herself or her ideas so much. The way she was acting now was highly unusual. "I know what you think, Mother. You've made it very clear, and I'm trying hard to believe you."

Knowingly her mother shrugged her shoulders. "I think one of the things that might be troubling you is that you find Brooks an attractive distraction. Lord knows all the other women I've met do."

"Not you too!" Lindee fairly shouted. "Every woman around here acts as if he were the only man alive." Then she shook her head, calming herself. "He's attractive all right, but hardly my type."

"Oh, my dear, I heartily disagree. I think you're very much alike." She caught a glimpse of Lindee's hostile frown. "All right, Lindee," her mother said with a hint of a sigh. "I've got to go, but I know, I just know you'll make the right decision. We're counting on you."

Her words couldn't have been better planned, Lindee realized, watching her mother quietly go through the door. She was playing on her daughter's sense of responsibility and fairness. She'd known exactly what she was doing. If Lindee continued to insist upon Brooks's exclusion, she would, in essence, be telling her staff that they were all wrong, that their judgments weren't good enough for her. And both Vivian and her daughter knew that in the long run Lindee simply could not go against them all in that way. She was far too loyal for that.

Opening the door a half inch, Lindee called, "Mother, I'll retract my request. Brooks Griffin can stay with my campaign." There didn't seem to be any other choice. "I'll tell Earl."

"Oh, darling, you're making the right decision. I'm sure of it," her mother insisted. "I'll tell Earl myself. And the television interview? You are going to do that, too, aren't you?"

"Yes. Good-bye, Mother." Lindee sighed and closed the door. All her options were effectively stopped for now. But she'd stay away from Brooks Griffin. That was all she could do.

A rush of sadness seized her then, sadness for the friends it seemed she never had time for anymore, the intimacy of relationships. She was lonely, but that feeling was to be expected. She'd been warned by any number of seasoned politicians before. Only now it seemed more real than she'd ever dared imagine.

33

After a quick shower she dialed Earl's room. "Earl, I'm going to do a little quick shopping this morning while I have a chance. I need a few things—like a good book to help me get to sleep at night, and apples—I'm out of apples."

Earl's laugh sounded into the telephone. It was a joke with everybody the way she ate apples. Apples and pantyhose, her campaign couldn't go on without those two things.

Pushing aside the thoughts that were plaguing her, Lindee dressed in a pair of jeans and a green silk blouse. She pulled her hair back, secured it at her nape with three strong bobby pins, and grabbed a pair of dark sunglasses. Shopping trips were rare nowadays, and she looked forward to this break in the campaign routine.

Closing the door behind her, she adjusted her sunglasses. Mentally she was planning where she'd go and what she'd do. There was a dress shop that she wanted to visit if she had time, but she decided she'd wait and make up her mind as she went along. Everything else in her life was structured right now. She had two hours of freedom.

"Good morning," Brooks's voice cut through to her.

She couldn't believe it. "What now?" she asked impatiently.

"Didn't you get my message this morning? I want to talk to you before the interview," he explained.

It was then that he looked at her with those unusual dark eyes, and her insides suddenly felt a little like putty. The silence that ensued between them was agonizingly long, but she forced herself to wait him out; besides, she could think of nothing to say. She was too astonished at the odd sensations that were racing pell-mell along every nerve in her body.

The moments dragged on as they stood in the hall. Then Brooks broke the silence. "Lindee, I'd like to apologize for last night. If I offended you in any way I'm sorry." His tone was appeasing, but there was a hint of resistance there, as if he were reading each word from a teleprompter, apologizing because he had to, not because he believed he should.

"Mr. Griffin, I'm going to accept your apology, if that's what it is. And I hope you understand it's against my better judgment, but I'm warning you I'll tolerate nothing like that again. Now if you'll excuse me." She began walking toward the elevator.

"Wait," he said, catching up with her. "Where are you going? To have your hair done for the television cameras this afternoon?"

Self-consciously she reached up and touched her hair. "No," she retorted. "I am not." She hadn't thought her hair looked that bad.

"Let me guess," he went on, holding the elevator door open for her. "Shopping? That's it."

She leaned against the back wall of the elevator, unwilling to look at him, her jaw set in anger. She didn't have to talk to him until the interview, she told herself.

Brooks paid no attention to the way she was behaving. He'd expected as much, but that hadn't stopped him from wanting to see her. He was taking a big chance right now, but if everything went his way, he'd have a few minutes alone with her, and that was all he needed. He had to have this time. She was driving him to distraction. "I've got something to show you," he told her, a soft smile playing at the corners of his mouth.

It made her furious that he was trying to manipulate her this way, and succeeding as well. "Show it to my campaign manager first. Everything goes through him," she snapped.

Before she could say another word or think another thought the elevator stopped on the second floor and Brooks took her wrist and pulled her out the door with him. She didn't regain her senses for a few seconds and by then he was propelling her down another hallway.

"Stop this," she demanded.

"Okay." He opened a door, and tightening his grip on her arm, he led her inside what appeared to be a small private meeting room.

Near the windows that looked out on the city was a solitary table with a white linen tablecloth laden with two plates, two cups, silver serving pieces, and a bouquet of fresh flowers. Any

35

other time, with any other man, it would have been charmingly romantic.

"What do you think you're doing?" She turned back to look at him, her hands on her hips, full of an anger that was becoming customary whenever he was around.

"I thought we'd have breakfast. I've got hot coffee, freshly squeezed orange juice, and the best blueberry muffins in all of Cowtown. Eat breakfast with me, and I'll leave you alone. Scout's honor," he said, holding up two fingers and at the same time pulling out the chair for her.

"Who else is coming?" she asked, warily looking around the beautifully appointed room.

"You and I don't need anyone else." He watched for her reaction, and seeing that he was making her nervous, he changed his mood. "Just kidding. Sit down. All I want is for the two of us to have breakfast alone. I told Earl and Steve that we needed a few minutes for a preliminary session before the interview. That's fair, isn't it?" He motioned her toward the chair.

"I suppose," she answered, not certain at all that it was fair. But maybe he did have a point. Rehearsing the questions might make for a better interview later. "But you have the worst manners I've ever seen in a reporter."

"Coffee?" he offered. Seeing her shake her head, he poured a large glass of orange juice and put a steaming hot muffin on her plate with a sliver of butter. He watched her now—the way her body had frozen for a brief second when she'd realized that they were all alone.

"So, what do you want to discuss?" she ventured as she sipped the juice.

"Why don't you ever look me straight in the eye when I talk to you? You do everyone else I see you talking to. And why do you pretend you don't like me when you know you do? And last but not least, when could we go out together? Tonight?" The words fell in rapid-fire succession, without pause until he was finished.

A piece of the muffin lodged in her throat and she coughed

once. "Is this what you wanted to talk about?" she asked in astonishment. "Of all the gall."

"Wait, wait." He put his hand over hers, afraid she was going to get up. "I do have some important questions to ask you."

"Well, you've got about five seconds." She had to take a sip of orange juice to clear her throat, but all the time her brain was registering the way his hand lay on top of hers. "Let's hear your questions."

"I heard you'd been engaged once. Is that true? The public will be interested in knowing."

Why was it that he always seemed to be enjoying himself, and it was entirely at her expense, this video prima donna? He smiled across the table as if they were the best of friends. "I'd rather not talk about that this afternoon, if you don't mind," she said dryly. "What about issues?"

"Okay." He agreed to oblige her, but he knew and she did, too, that he was a man who switched tactics in his interviews, slicing away layer by layer, looking for some bit of information no one else had discovered.

"We'll discuss anything you want to discuss. You just tell me what you want. Right now I'm interested in the way your face reveals your every emotion. That's not too good for a politician. Don't you know that?"

His words wrapped themselves around her intriguingly. He didn't come right out and say what he wanted, but he never let up on her. She could feel the enormous attraction of the man, but she could also feel the danger. "Thanks for the orange juice and the muffin. I have to go," she said, getting up.

"See, it wasn't so bad being alone with me, was it?" he teased as he walked her to the door, holding her elbow in his hand. "Maybe tonight we can try again."

"We won't be trying anything, Mr. Griffin, unless it's strictly professional."

"Don't be so sure, Lindee. Don't be so sure," he said softly before bending down to brush his lips across hers. And then, without another word, he ushered her out of the door and closed it between them.

For a long time she stood in the hallway, staring at the door, hardly realizing she had let herself be kissed. Slowly she walked to the elevator, wondering what she'd done to deserve this kind of complication in her life right now.

But after she'd had time to reflect on it, she had to laugh at herself. Brooks Griffin was determined to let nothing stand in the way of his own career. He'd as much as told her that. What was it she'd overheard him say yesterday to someone on her staff? "I learned a long time ago that you've got to think fast and on your feet if you want to stay alive in this business, and if you want to get ahead you've got to show everybody you're not afraid to lead the pack."

She was to be his target. That was the only explanation for his doggedly persistent pursuit of her. He wanted to be a part of her campaign, center stage. That way he could help Bullock, distract her, and keep himself in the spotlight. Well, she wouldn't be so easy to distract, she vowed. And at the same time she told herself it would do her no good to acknowledge the faint stirring of differing emotions he'd aroused. That he was an attractive man who'd reminded her that she was a woman was not to be denied, but she told herself to forget his enticing words and suggestive ways. Nothing about him should interest her.

He'd taken all the fun out of her shopping trip, and by the time she returned she could think of only one thing—the upcoming interview. She'd use it to show Brooks Griffin just how strong a candidate she really was.

Carefully she chose the dress she would wear. She had to make up her mind what sort of image she wanted to project, and she discarded several dresses before she came to the right one. Most of them were too dressy for an afternoon interview, while one or two of them were a bit too plain for a statewide television audience. Once she considered wearing pants and a silk blouse, but as quickly as she thought about it she changed her mind. She was a woman, and it was best to let everyone be certain of that fact.

38

Finally she selected a simple silk shirtwaist, light taupe in color and deceptively nondescript. Her choice, she knew, was a good one. It did nothing to distract from her looks. Viewers would look at her face, not her clothes.

Taking extra pains with her makeup and especially her hair, she ate a stale tuna sandwich ordered up from room service while she applied the finishing touches. It was almost one o'clock and she was determined she wouldn't be late.

Slipping into a pair of leather heels that blended nicely with her dress, she glanced up into the mirror over the dresser. Her reflection stared back at her. With a laugh to herself she decided that if her mother were with her she'd insist that Lindee apply a great deal more makeup, but that was entirely out of character for Lindee. She didn't like the harsh look heavy makeup gave her.

Imbued with a great deal of common sense as well as intelligence, Lindee knew she was attractive, certainly not beautiful, not even strikingly pretty, but attractive to those who chose to look her way. She had a face that people remembered, a look that was appealing, and a figure to match. When she wanted to, Lindee could be as glamorous as the next woman, and the media called her a "sophisticated lady."

She had never been interested in the false beauty that money could buy. She liked her looks. Maybe they weren't the kind that took every man's breath away, but she'd never felt the need some women had to be on display all the time, no matter what the price. She was as comfortable with the way she looked as she was with the way she felt and where she was going.

Earl was knocking at the door when she sprayed her wrists with a mist of light perfume, and he gave her a brotherly hug when she opened the door. Brooks's voice could be heard, issuing orders to the cameramen already out on the veranda. Earl silently mouthed words for good luck while she quickly slipped past him and made her way to the outside, taking little notice of anything other than the man whom she was to meet once again.

In the back of her mind she'd pictured him getting his notes together, or combing his hair, or perhaps straightening his tie, concentrating on his television appearance. Instead she found him leaning out across the railing, taking in the sights and sounds of the city. His dark hair was rumpled, his tie hung slightly off center, and he had a look of relaxed calm that she envied.

"I assume you're ready, Mr. Griffin," she said as she walked toward him. "Are we to sit or stand? And how long do you think this will last?" She sounded every bit the political candidate.

His mouth twisted in a mocking grin as he acknowledged her attempt to show him who was in control. "Let's begin where we are right now. I assume you want to get on with it."

She leaned back against the railing, letting her hair blow around her face. It was too late to worry about it now. Anything she might suggest would seem too inflexible. "Certainly," she said.

"Okay, Mike, turn her on," he called over his shoulder.

Suddenly Brooks was standing between Lindee and the camera blocking out the heat and the harsh glare of the lights, and she could hear his voice booming into the microphone. She could literally feel the intensity of the man as he stood with his back to her, his bearing controlled and totally self-confident. Mesmerized at first by the powerful way he had of playing to the camera, she stood utterly still.

Then he slowly turned his head, giving her his full attention. Everyone at WBCX had predicted he could really make headline news with the woman who stood next to him. As for himself, he hadn't decided yet. If she was as complex as she appeared to be, he was in for a real challenge. Already he'd found himself having a hard time focusing on his work. His pulse raced, and he could almost feel the adrenaline surge through him. She was the most unnerving distraction he'd ever seen. Nothing had ever pulled him away from his work like this before.

Brooks loved his job, and the next few minutes with Lindee promised to be more than a little exciting. He wondered if the chemistry between them would be noticeable on the screen, and he told himself to be cool. He was a prize-winning performer, and letting her interfere with his job was inconceivable.

"Miss Bradley, you're a candidate for the Texas senate, running against one of the strongest names in our state's political arena. You're a woman, that's going to be a strike against you, and you're unmarried, and very young for this job if your biographers are correct in reporting your age as thirty. How can you possibly believe you can win this election—or don't you?"

Momentarily taken back by the hostility implied by his questions, she almost flinched, but her determination overrode her feelings of panic. This man was shrewdly twisting his questions so that she was on the defensive. It wasn't going to be a friendly interview at all.

"First of all, Mr. Griffin," she said, pushing away the strands of hair that lightly swirled around her face, "I *am* thirty years old, and while that may seem young to many there's my record of serving as an assistant district attorney in San Antonio and my past service on any number of state and local boards and committees. I can assure you and the citizens of this great state that I have had a great deal of practical experience in serving the people. For those who say I can't beat a man who's been around as long as Mr. Bullock, well, if this campaign is fought on the issues, I think I can win hands down." A self-satisfied smile touched her lips. She'd forgotten all about their being before the cameras now. All that really mattered was getting her points across to this aggressive man who insisted upon challenging her every word.

"What makes you think you can win on issues?" he shot back before she could catch her breath.

"I'm confident that the voters aren't interested in a personality contest. I sincerely believe that they are educated and well aware of what's important to them and to their families."

He aimed question after question in rapid-fire succession. He'd done his homework well because he knew exactly what he wanted to ask and how to ask it.

"Do you think being raised in a wealthy family hurts your chances of identifying with the average voter?"

She opened her mouth to respond, but already he was blurting out the next question.

"Do you know anyone, I mean intimately, who isn't wealthy?"

"Of course I do." Her eyes lit up with animosity. Brooks knew her record; he knew the reputation she'd established for helping others. How dare he? "Naturally I do, and I don't want the viewers to misunderstand this. I am not a wealthy woman who's never worked for a living. I have worked steadily since the day I left law school."

"But you've grown up in an atmosphere of wealth, and later this year you will have access to a trust fund that was bequeathed to you. Correct?"

"Yes, that's right, and while it's perhaps more money than many people have, it's certainly not going to put me in the category of the wealthy."

"That depends on your definition," he stated flatly.

She held her tongue. Any response right now would only be twisted to make his point. Better to just let it pass. Bravely she maintained her serene expression, but her mind raced with resentment.

"Why do you want to be a state senator, Miss Bradley?"

"Why? Because I know that I can serve the people and represent their interests and not special interest groups like the oil or the cattle industry."

Instinctively he reacted. "And yet, Miss Bradley, those on the inside of the political scene say that your supporters, your major contributors, are some of those very people, rich cattlemen and oilmen, people embroiled in every part of corporate Texas. What do you say to that?"

She should have known. He grinned at her, obviously thinking he'd caught her again. They both remembered the pictures of her on television with the likes of P. J. Johnson, a man who owned more oil wells than any other individual in the world.

"Yes, I have a few, but if you'd bother to look at the difference

42

in contributions to my campaign and that of Mr. Bullock's you could tell right away that the vast majority of my contributions are from Bexar County. On the other hand, Mr. Bullock's financial statements reveal that over ninety percent of his contributions came from the cattle and oil industries. His past voting record substantiates all of this."

"Some people say you're trying to ride in on the memory of your father. He was a state senator for many years. Is that true?"

"It's true he was a state senator, but it's not true that I'm trying to ride on his memory. How could that be so when he's been dead for twelve years?" She turned so that she was directly facing him. This was getting to be fun, now that she'd found out how the game was played. The thrill of the unspoken contest that was going on between the two of them was uplifting, undeniably exciting.

Predictably, he switched his line of questioning for a moment. "How's all this going to affect your personal life, Miss Bradley? You do have a social life? Correct me if I'm wrong."

"If you mean . . ." she began. Then, warning herself that this might be a setup, she proceeded to answer him cautiously. "If you mean social life as far as friends and all, I'm afraid that the campaign hasn't enabled me to be around my close friends as much as I'd like, but I manage to keep in touch."

He leaned toward her, baiting her with his next question. "I've been told by a close personal friend of yours that you have no time for your friends or for dating. Is that true?"

"Right now I have only one goal. I intend to be elected to the state senate on November fourth. That leaves me little time for anything else." She tried to maintain her composure, but he was getting to her with his prying.

"The public wants to know all about you. Is it true that you were engaged to be married and a few weeks before the wedding your fiancé broke it off?"

"What does that have to do with my running for office?" she exploded. He'd gone too far, and for the life of her she wished she'd never seen him, never even heard of him. Visibly shaken,

43

she longed to storm away from him and even considered doing just that. Then she saw the look of utter dismay on Earl's face, and she realized she was making a terrible mistake.

"Stop, please," she said, looking over at Brooks, who stood warily eyeing her. "Wait, if you could erase that part of the tape, I'd like to continue, but I'd prefer that you restrict your questions to my public life." Her breathing came in shallow gasps. Right now he was in control. If he chose to, he could refuse her request and that might be fatal to the campaign. She'd made a near tragic mistake, responding with her emotions instead of her head, and her facial expression had been captured by the camera.

"Okay." He nodded, acting as though nothing had happened. "Mike, we'll go back to where Miss Bradley said, 'That leaves me little time for anything else.' "

They sat down at the small wrought-iron table, their chairs so near each other that when the camera started up again she could feel his knee brushing against her leg. Oddly, it didn't disturb her. And his attitude had changed, maybe not to that of a casual observer, but he seemed aware that he'd crossed a very personal line with her. She knew his next comment would be perfectly courteous and gracious.

He looked at her for a long moment before rephrasing his question. "Now, Miss Bradley, the public wants to know more about you, the woman. I assume that at some time or another you've entertained the thought of getting married, and if you have, what kind of effect might it have if you were to marry while serving in office?"

She almost laughed. She had to hand it to him. He'd gotten around her initial objection, and still he jumped right back in there, able to innocently ask her in a roundabout way the question he'd intended all along.

"Yes, I've thought of getting married. I've even come close a few times, but right now I have no man in my life. And . . ."—she looked directly into the camera and managed a cool smile—"I am certain that nothing would interfere with my job performance."

"I would think dating, things like that, would take up a great deal of time," he persisted.

"Mr. Griffin, would you be asking the same kind of questions if I were a man? I don't think so." She shook her head before looking into the camera again and speaking further. "I will be able to handle anything that comes my way, I'm certain. Believe me, nothing would interfere with my service to the people of Texas, and particularly Bexar County." Her eyes sparkled and she flashed a wide girlish grin into the lens, hoping with all her might that the sincerity of her words would be reflected in her face.

"Thank you, Miss Bradley, for agreeing to talk to us today. It's been a real revelation." He let his eyes brush across her face before he looked at the camera. "I'm sure we'll be doing more interviews like this in the next few days. I look forward to that." The rest of his words were lost to her as he began winding up the segment for the news staff.

When the camera lights were turned off it was a sudden sensation like cooling down on a beach somewhere. She stayed where she was, telling herself to relax for a second.

"Champagne," Earl shouted. His arms were full of glasses and bottles of champagne. Quickly he passed them around, first to Lindee and then to Brooks before turning to the others. "A special toast to a wonderful lady," he enthused. "You were fabulous."

She knew it, too, and she also knew that part of the credit belonged to Brooks. The electricity between them kept her on her toes, alert and freshly spontaneous, but there had been moments when it had been like a living nightmare.

Realizing she wasn't through with the man who'd led her through the tortuous interview, she grabbed a bottle of champagne from Earl's arm as he passed by and spoke directly to Brooks, keeping her voice soft and low. She didn't want him to leave just yet.

"Brooks, won't you stay and have another drink with me? I'd like to talk with you."

His lips lingered over the champagne glass as he studied her then, and unexpectedly he nodded. "You know that I've been wanting that, too, just the two of us."

She waited to make certain they were alone before she said anything more. Already she felt more relaxed. The tension of the interview was over. Now she could regain some sense of control over her life, and the first thing she was going to do was let him know his limits.

"I'm curious," she began softly. "Why is it that you're so interested in me?"

His eyebrows shot up in surprise. He hadn't expected her bluntness. Pouring himself another glassful from the champagne bottle on the table, he sipped at it before answering. "There's a definite attraction between us," he answered honestly. His eyes took in every part of her from the tips of her leather shoes to the crown of her fiery chestnut hair. As he conducted his cool appraisal she watched his every move, but he didn't bother to conceal his appreciation, letting his provocative gaze stay a little too long on the steady rise and fall of her breasts and then on her lips.

Her voice was strongly compelling when she spoke. "I think you're deluding yourself. What I'm feeling is animosity. Do you know the meaning of the word?" She lifted her head high. "And what you've been doing with my campaign is obvious enough. Last night's incident was ridiculous, and your questions today were hostile and degrading. They didn't turn out to have quite that impact, but through no fault of your own. What's your next trick? I'd like to know."

As though they weren't at odds with each other, he slowly unknotted his tie, refilled her glass, and then leaned calmly back in his chair. With a deliberately mocking smile he spoke, but not until he was good and ready. It drove her insane, this casual insolence of his.

"First of all, I want to say that you were brilliant today. I've got to confess you surprised me. Secondly, you've got to be an idiot . . ." he let the words sink in, "if you really think that my joining this spirited little campaign of yours hasn't been beneficial. Hell, Lindee, both of us can profit from this." He ran his fingers through his hair and tilted his head toward her, his body never once evidencing the exasperation he was feeling. "So far I've been doing what I consider to be a very good job. Look, I get what I want and you get what you want. Maybe I get a shot at a national news job and maybe you get a shot at being Texas's newest freshman senator. One hand washes the other."

Enraged as much by his show of indifference as by what he said, she knew only that she wanted to hurt him, to do anything to fight off the stinging blaze of fury that raced uncontrollably inside her. They were talking about two different things. "I've put up with about all I'm going to. Now, my campaign people want you to stay on, and I've agreed, but I want you to stay as far away from me as possible. Your brand of publicity is not anything I personally want," she demanded indignantly.

He reached out and grasped her arm. "You're wrong. Because if you don't want it, you sure as hell should. My God, woman, I just gave you an interview that will give your campaign more publicity than any of your staff could have gotten for you if they'd worked day and night for two weeks. Don't you think people are going to remember your name this way? I've given you a unique opportunity—one you ought to be grateful for instead of acting like I'd committed a felony. Look, Lindee, I know what I'm doing. I'm on my way up. Why would I start making mistakes now?"

Bitterly she said, "I don't believe you." And then another thought struck her. "If I'm wrong, why did you bother to apologize this morning? I don't see someone like you telling anyone he's sorry." She looked down to watch the way his grip had become a caress. He was lightly running his fingertips up and down along the soft inside part of her arm, sending an unfamiliar shiver to the edges of her spine.

"What did I apologize for? For flirting with you or making you angry? What exactly did I say?" he answered with a short laugh that held the faintest wisp of mystery as well as laughter.

"I'm a man of principles. Oh, but then you can't be convinced of that." He waited for a split second before going on, his eyes reproaching her far better than any of his words could. "But the news business is sometimes like politics. Compromise—that's the name of the game. I wanted to stay around you, see what's going to happen in the next couple of weeks, and I was willing to do whatever it took to convince you to let me stay." He watched her. "Who knows, maybe you and I can get some fun out of this. Maybe we'll even end up helping each other. Like I keep telling you, I'm trying my best."

"Is that the only reason?" she persisted.

There was a flicker of light that caught and danced in his eyes when he answered. "The only one I'm willing to give you right now." Breaking the spell that had existed between them, he urged her, "Drink your champagne, because I can see that you're not willing to listen to anything I might have to say about the subject of publicity." Casually he ran his fingers through his hair then, as if with one motion he could rebuff the anger she was sending his way.

"I am going to say one final thing, though." He laughed, more at himself than at anything else. "I bet old Earl is dancing a tango over the way our interview went today. Whether you want to admit it or not, Lindee, I was able to allow you to respond to some of the most often asked questions about you and your life. You virtually had a free forum to air your answers to all the questions that will be leveled against you."

Despite herself she had to admit his logic was more and more convincing. But his heavy-handed treatment was still gnawing at her. No matter what he might say or do, she couldn't quite bring herself to believe in him. Not when it was so evident to her that he was intent upon using her to further his own career.

"Why do you use such a demeaning tone of voice when you talk to me? Answer that," she charged.

"That's my style. I have to come on strong when I'm on camera. I believe it gets better answers from the people I'm interviewing. Remember, all of you politicians are pros at answering questions in a roundabout manner. You've had many, many interviews before I ever get to you."

"All in the interest of good reporting, is that it?"

"There's nothing wrong with good reporting. In fact, there are some who admire my reporting style." He smiled, and it changed his face, giving him that boyish allure that she'd seen projected so many times on camera. It was unnerving, the way he looked at her, so insatiably direct, as if he could overcome all her objections if she'd only let him.

"I'm sure," Lindee said sarcastically.

"Now," he insisted, "why don't we talk about something interesting? Your accusations are too much for an old country boy like me to deal with." He never took his eyes away from hers, made no movement, or said another word, but he'd managed to change the atmosphere between them, if only for a moment.

She had to laugh. Unable to sustain the intensity of her own emotions, aware of how he was masterfully diffusing her feelings with his very own special mixture of charm and verbal maneuvers, she had to confess that he'd been effective. Yet surely, she reassured herself, he'd got her message—for the time being, anyway.

She'd have to watch him, but at least he'd understood what she'd been telling him, and besides, she'd silently vowed to Earl and all the others that she'd try to deal with Brooks, and she couldn't go back on her promise so soon. Laughing again, a little self-consciously this time, she said, "You've a way about you, I have to admit. Somehow I bet you could convince the governor that he ought to let you into his bedroom, cameras and all."

He returned her laugh and set his glass down. "I don't know that I'm that persuasive, but if you'd like to give it a try yourself, I'd sure be willing to test my powers on you."

Again the smallest of shivers began at the base of her spine and wove its way through her the moment his words were spoken. He had the damnable ability to catch her off guard with his insinuations. It had happened over and over. She refused to allow her eyes to meet his.

Scornfully she changed her voice as well as the subject. "Why did you keep referring to my coming from a wealthy family during our interview? Would you be honest and answer that question?"

"No reason, actually, except that sometimes I don't believe money and politics should be so carefully interwoven. I don't begrudge you the money, Lindee. I merely believe that sometimes people who've been pampered all their lives don't have the opportunity to build character. They don't have to deal with much of anything other than the pursuit of pleasure."

"How did you grow up, Brooks? You look like a man who had all the advantages." She had listened to the tone of his voice, low and reassuring. Then her own words echoed in her ears. *The way I said his name you'd think we were old friends,* she thought. She had no idea how long they'd been sitting together. He still held her arm, only now his fingers only rested on the tenderest part of her wrist. Strangely, she realized, she didn't want this to end. It didn't make any difference that she didn't trust him, or that he'd been so awful to her. Suddenly, everything he had to say had become important to her.

"If you're really interested in knowing, yes, I had a great number of advantages. Maybe not the kind you're thinking about, but definite advantages. Next question?" His eyes had such a hard, determined look about them that she hesitated before saying anything else.

Knowing she couldn't allow herself to succumb to his seductive ways, she was nevertheless enjoying herself. "Go on."

"Enough about me. Let's go back to your original question. I want to say something else. Rich people in politics always bother me, Lindee. I don't quite trust them."

"But why?" she argued.

"A good many of them are shallow pleasure seekers, ready to give in to the first signs of corruption or opposition that stand in their way. They can't go the distance, that's all. Except for a few self-made men I've seen." His face was flushed with his emotions. He could hardly believe himself. She'd gotten him to open up with his own private views, while all the time he'd been solitarily intent upon uncovering hers.

"You really do respect power, don't you?" It was more a confirmation than a question. She studied his face, trying to read all that was stored there.

"Yes, I respect the people who have the courage to step out there and take chances. I admire that kind of power—internal power."

A slowly dawning awareness came over her. "You don't think I can beat Ted Bullock because you think I'm a loser. You see me as one of those kinds of people you were talking about."

He stared at her, revealing not the slightest hint of what he might be thinking. How in the hell could he possibly explain why he thought Bullock needed one more term in office? Lindee was simply too embroiled in the race to be able to stand back and take a look using his own objective viewpoint. He knew Bullock wasn't the man of the hour when it came to politics. Bullock had made some shady deals in the past, he was sure of it, but despite all that, the old man had sponsored a women's rights bill that would be the model for every state in the union to follow. But first he had to win one final election.

Earl's voice shattered the intimate connection between them. "Say, Brooks, I didn't thank you before. The interview was great. We just saw the videotape of it. She came across as the best candidate I've seen in a long time. Thanks." Earl nodded to both of them and stepped back into the hotel suite.

A long period of silence rested between them. Once again the mood had changed, but Lindee desperately wanted to force him to answer her last question.

He stood up and she held out a hand to stop him. "Tell me, do you believe I can beat Ted Bullock or not?"

"Another time," he promised huskily. "Another time."

"No, now." She touched his arm and felt the pressure of his resistance. Then he pulled her to him.

"You're going to have to learn two things, lady. One thing is that you can't always have your way whenever you want it." His

51

voice was rawly disturbing and he held her much too near him, his arm wrapped around her waist. "Secondly, by being fair and impartial I'm actually trying to help you on this glorious campaign of yours, not hurt you."

"Help me?" she flared, shocked back into reality by his voice. "I think you're confused. Helping yourself is what you're doing."

They struggled then; he refused to let her go. And when she stood still again, in agonizingly slow motion he bent down, sliding his hand up from the small of her back to linger just at the softest part of her neck. She sensed the pressure of his fingertips urging her face nearer to his, and when she lifted her eyes she caught sight of a trace of gentleness in his eyes that hadn't been there before.

She told herself to push away from this contradictory man, but when his lips met hers she gave herself a little more time. She wasn't a schoolgirl, and handling a kiss from an attractive man wasn't difficult at all.

But neither was this a schoolboy's kiss, for when his lips met hers there was no trace of innocence or gentle persuasion. Instead, she opened her mouth in response to a demanding fervor that caught her unaware. That was the only reason her mind could provide for the shaky response she felt, and the undeniable rush of pleasure that overwhelmed her when his tongue began to explore the hidden recesses of her mouth.

He crushed her against him, one arm pressing the small of her back, the other pulling her neck forward so that her lips were there to claim his. His mouth parted her lips with a desire that needed no words. The mere touch of his body pressing against her evoked a feeling that she was at a loss to explain. She'd kept those kinds of thoughts far back in her mind, setting her sights for something other than physical pleasure so very long ago.

His hands roamed up and down her body, coming to rest along the jutting curve of her breast, and then he ran the palm of his warm hand across her nipple, arousing inside her a decided warmth that she knew she should fight against.

Brooks kissed her hungrily, and his hands were crazed with the need to touch her, as if through this physical contact he could find out all there was to know about her, prove to himself that everything he might think about her was true. But Lindee Bradley was too complex for so simple a definition, and when she pulled away he was aware of it with a knowledge that burned through the deepest part of him.

"I'm glad we're going to be together," he murmured, brushing his lips against her forehead, accepting her reluctance. Gently he stroked her arm with the lightest caress.

"We're not . . ."

"Don't tell me what we're not going to do," he cautioned before his voice softened again. "Just this once, let your emotions go, lady. Feel, don't think." He started to reach for her again.

"Don't, Brooks."

"Okay," he whispered. "But answer one question for me. Are we going to work together instead of against each other?" His lips traced a tender outline across hers. "I've told you all along, there's something special between us."

A funny feeling welled up inside her. In a distant voice she answered, "We can try to work together, but you didn't have to kiss me. It wasn't necessary."

He didn't know whether she was being humorous or cool. Either way, he had no way of finding out, because, ignoring his confused expression, she left him standing alone as she turned and walked back inside the hotel suite and softly shut the door of her bedroom behind her.

Away from his insinuating presence, Lindee told herself Brooks was a man who had climbed that precarious ladder of success at a speed far greater than any race track driver's. He was thirty-six years old, already famous throughout the state, an acknowledged master of his craft as well as being a recognized television personality. Now why in the world would he suddenly find her so interesting? It had to be that he only wanted to profit himself, his own career. Right now she made good copy. He was thinking of her as his very own personal headline maker, another way to skip a few rungs on that long ladder.

Well, she was a woman on her way up, too, and her emotions were never, never, absolutely *never* going to get in her way. She had dreams. Big ones. And they didn't include becoming involved with a man she dare not trust.

She leaned against the cold, hard surface of the door, hands pressed against her eyes. "Too much is happening, too fast," she murmured. "You're exhausted, Lindee," she excused herself. "Now forget that man and get back to the business at hand. Save yourself."

CHAPTER THREE

The outside air was choked with blowing dust. Through the window of the airplane Lindee could feel the grit when it struck metal like tiny pebbles thudding against glass. Lindee pressed her forehead against the cool inner wall of the plane, reacting to the sensation of the engine's vibrations with the crazy sense of freedom that she could always find this high above the clouds.

The hectic pace of the last couple of days had been maddening; too fast, too terribly demanding. She felt as if she'd been drained of her last drop of energy after the series of whirlwind luncheons with every women's club in the county, and all those early morning meetings with everyone of voting age, from the Elks Lodge to the employees of a Jack-in-the-Box who had graciously served her hot coffee and a breakfast roll early one morning. Now, flying into the state capital of Austin, she wondered why she'd agreed to come. She needed to be back in San Antonio working with the voters.

As if the political part of her life hadn't been demanding enough, there had been the problem with Brooks. She'd realized as soon as they'd parted that late afternoon two days ago that she'd made an error in judgment when she'd let him kiss her, and most especially when she'd found herself beginning to care about his opinions and ideas when they'd talked alone over the bottle of bubbly champagne.

If she weren't so tired she could almost think it was funny—their coming together at such an impossible time in their lives. Timing—that was one of the biggest problems, because she wasn't dishonest enough to deny that she'd found him very appealing. Oh, but now was hardly the time for a major television reporter and an aspiring state senator to develop an interest in each other, she told herself. Besides all that, she had her own aspirations, just as he had his, and being with a man like Brooks, who found her interesting in direct proportion to her publicity value—well, she didn't need anything from him, neither his support nor his attentions. That was why she'd tried so hard to stay away from him. Better to close the door to the possibility than to pursue something that could only be fantasy and never reality.

The light flashed overhead, signaling the passengers to fasten their seat belts for landing. As fast as possible Lindee began grabbing up her typed notes, which lay scattered across both the empty seats beside her. Stuffing them into her briefcase, she reached for her purse, took out her cosmetics bag, and began rummaging around for her powder and lipstick. The plane was making its descent, and before she had time to brush her hair, Earl was standing beside her seat, checking to see if she were ready.

Quickly she unfastened her seat belt and stood up, smoothing down the lines of her dark blue suit. She knew her blouse was wrinkled, but there was nothing to be done about it. Weary travelers always had that rumpled look, she assured herself.

"Lindee, try not to give much time to the reporters waiting to greet you. We'll be bombarded by the media this afternoon after Bullock has his ten o'clock press conference. Save yourself for later." Earl reached out a hand to help her, offering to take her heavy briefcase for her, but she refused with a faint nod in his direction.

"You promised me I'd have two hours alone before the Chamber of Commerce speech." She frowned, recalling how she'd been invited, along with one other woman running for state office, to speak about the woman's role in Texas politics. She still wasn't sure she should have come, but Earl had insisted it would be good publicity. "Don't forget that, Earl. It's all that's kept me going this morning after only four and a half hours of sleep, knowing I'd have some private time to take care of some of my personal business."

"You'll get it. Don't worry," he insisted as they walked down the aisle and out into the airport terminal.

Earl pushed her past the cluster of local newspeople who stood in the lobby. Smiling and shaking hands with as many of her well-wishers as she could, Lindee felt her spirits improve. There was nothing like the thrill of the crowd. She loved it like nothing else she'd ever experienced. It kept her going, charged up her spirits.

"Tired, aren't you?" Brooks spoke so softly that only she could hear him. He was standing just to her left side.

"Where did you come from?" she asked, still smiling and waving to the onlookers.

"We reporters always manage to be where the action is." His voice was light and teasing, matching his wide grin.

"Yes, that's true," Lindee answered resignedly.

"Why don't we go on to the hotel, just you and I. We can talk for a while before your speech at noon. I promise I won't mention politics, not even once." It was the first chance he'd had to talk to her in two days.

He followed her step for step as Earl led the way to the car that waited for them. Out of all the thoughts that danced through her head there was one that stayed with her, if only for a minisecond. She wondered, merely wondered, what would happen if she said yes and raced to the nearest exit with him, leaving everyone behind.

"Thanks, but no, thanks. I have lots of work to do." She didn't look at him when she answered.

"You're trying to avoid me, but I warn you, I refuse to be put

57

off." She could hear the humor in the way he spoke to her. She knew he wasn't offended by her refusal, but she believed he meant what he said, and it made her want to smile.

Brooks watched her as she got into the back seat of the sedan, and when the car pulled away from the curb he wanted to call her name, talk to her just a little longer. She'd given him the cold shoulder ever since they'd talked on the day of the interview, but he could bide his time. A week was a long time for them to be together, and anything could happen.

But he knew one thing. He'd known it from the first, and every time he saw her he was reminded of his vow. He wanted her and, by damn, he was going to have her, come hell or high water. At first he'd been amused by her, then curious about her, and now there was the feeling of something more intense. Hating to admit he had feelings for her that he'd never had before, Brooks hailed a cab and got in, abruptly switching his thoughts. He had to call in to the television station and find out what Bullock was saying in his news conference.

Thirty minutes later Lindee was settled into a suite at the Holiday Inn near the site of the luncheon she was scheduled to attend that day. Earl had promised there would be no interruptions, and looking forward to the brief reprieve, she kicked off her shoes, fluffed up a pillow to use as a backrest, and tried to make herself comfortable on the bed. Unsuccessful, she tried again, taking off her clothes, pushing the pillow up against the headboard, and finally settling in before letting out a deep sigh of contentment.

She reached for her briefcase, took out an address book, and began to dial. When the voice on the other end of the line answered Lindee smiled. "Yolanda, this is Lindee. How are you?"

Yolanda Martinez was one of the strongest forces in the state political party. Ten years ago she'd been just a quiet housewife, unhappy with the way she thought things were being done to help the Mexican Americans in the barrios, poor sections of the city of San Antonio. Organizing a group of women neighbors, some of whom spoke little English, Yolanda Martinez had started one of the strongest political action groups in the state. She believed that someone should help the oppressed. She also believed in Lindee Bradley.

"Oh, Lindee, I'm so happy to hear from you. I saw you on television the other night. You looked great." Her bubbly personality brightened Lindee's day.

"Thank you, Yolanda. I haven't had a chance to call before now, and I've been thinking about you. How did your protest go with city hall?"

"Which one? Really, since we last talked together I have led two groups over two different issues." She laughed then. "I have a very hard time sometimes remembering exactly what I'm complaining about."

"I don't believe that for a second, my friend."

"You are right. I am only teasing. Both of the protests have caused the council to postpone any decisions. Everything's going as usual here, but it's not me I'm interested in talking about. It is you. From what I see I think your campaign is going very well."

"Yes, I think you're right. We've had a lot of good things happen for us lately, Yolanda, and I'm getting more and more excited. What I'm interested in knowing about is the voters in the barrio. What are they saying about the race? What are they most interested in?" The sincerity of her words underlined the importance of her question.

"Well, the poor people want you in office. They think you will be more sympathetic to their problems. They remember how you tried to help them save their community center. That was very important to my people."

Lindee thought back to the time she'd joined Yolanda's group in a march that demonstrated their protests against the destruction of a seventy-year-old building that had been the site of weddings and parties and neighborhood gatherings for as long as any of them could remember. It had been a very sentimental

59

issue. Yet for Lindee there were many such occasions to remember.

By the time she reached the age of thirty, Lindee Bradley had developed into the woman her father had predicted she would become. She was bright, articulate, and had an unflagging interest in helping people better their lives through the political process. As a lawyer her reputation had spread so far that she often received phone calls asking her to travel to this place or that to help out individuals who felt they needed someone who was considered a champion of human rights. For those people in need, the fact that she was a woman seemingly never interfered.

Respected by people in every station of life, Lindee had felt that now was the time to become even more involved in what she believed in. That was why she'd filed for the state senate race, telling her friends and family only after she'd officially become a candidate. Once she'd filed, her supporters had gathered around her in surprising numbers. Sometimes Lindee couldn't believe her own good fortune.

Saying good-bye to her friend, she hung up and called a few other people located in various parts of her district who offered advice and solicited hers. They, too, were people who believed in Lindee's cause. They'd seen her in action. Each one had been helped in one way or another by her, and it had always been done without a great deal of fanfare, but with just enough publicity so that everyone's cause was improved.

Knowing that her freedom was slipping away, Lindee glanced at her watch just as the phone rang. How had that much time gone by? she wondered.

"Hi, I hate to bother you. I know I promised you free time, but something's come up," Earl said. She could hear scattered voices in the background.

"What is it?"

He hesitated. "I think we'd better talk. Should I come to your room or do you want to come here?"

Reluctantly she said, "Whatever you think best."

"Okay, Steve and I will be there in a minute. Don't answer

your phone or the door. We'll knock twice when we come. Okay?"

"Why? Are the reporters after me or what?"

"You guessed it. Bullock's just laid a bombshell in our laps. Sit tight. We'll be right up."

She hung up the telephone receiver and without a moment's hesitation put on her clothes. There was no time to do anything about her makeup, but she pushed her fingers artfully through her long hair, restoring it to some semblance of order.

The signal came and Lindee answered the door, ushering in the two men, who looked as exhausted as she had felt earlier. Now that she'd had the time to make some of the personal connections that were so important to her she felt refreshed, and her face showed it.

"I'm glad you're looking better, Lindee, because we've got a problem," Earl said before sitting down on the rumpled bed.

"I figured that from the way you talked on the phone. What is it?" she answered, motioning for Steve to sit down wherever he could find a chair. She remained standing.

"Ted Bullock held his press conference at ten o'clock sharp." She nodded. That was common knowledge.

"Bullock said," Earl went on, his voice rising, "that he'd called the press conference just to let the voters know, particularly all the women voters of the state . . . that his bill for women's rights was picking up interest all over the country." Earl shook his head. "He went on to tell how good it was. He bragged for about fifteen minutes, saying that would be his first priority in the next session of the legislature. You know what a windbag he can be."

Lindee nodded her agreement. Now was not the time to interrupt Earl. She could just imagine his fidgeting impatience when he'd had to listen to Bullock rattle on.

"Bullock said, very dramatically, I might add, that he'd been waiting for some statement, some sign from his worthy opponent that she, too, supported his women's rights bill. He went on and on, Lindee, saying that women voters and all of those who care about this great state of ours should vote for him. It was clear, he said, that not only could you not be counted on to support women's rights, you obviously couldn't be counted on for support of any major issue. You just wanted to get elected."

She looked at him in wide-mouthed astonishment. "Well, well, well, is he ever trying to stir up a hornet's nest!" It all sounded preposterous, but from the looks on their faces this was no laughing matter.

"The bad thing about it, Lindee, is that you and I both know that bill is a real wonder. It's said to have all the best features of any rights bill written, and the bad things are all deleted. It's practically perfect." Earl's face was white. "You're going to catch heat for not taking a stand on this—one way or another. Bullock's going to see to it."

Lindee sighed. She should have expected something like this.

"And that's not all," Earl went on breathlessly. "That man compared you to a girl wanting to make sure she had a date for the prom, telling four different guys she'd go with them and then choosing when they all got there. He told the reporters that you were the kind of candidate who went around telling every group exactly what they wanted to hear, while not actually supporting anything. And then . . ." He paused. "And then he said you'd let bipartisan politics kill the women's rights bill and then you'd throw the last scoop of dirt in as they bury it."

"How dare he?" she fumed. Pacing the floor she couldn't contain her feelings of outrage. "How dare he take a cheap shot like that? Frightened . . . he's got to be frightened. That's the only possible explanation."

"You're right, Lindee, of course, but now what do you want to do about it? He finally said that the women of Texas were going to be shortchanged if you won the election." Earl's own sense of anger had returned. His face had turned beet red, and he'd wadded up the notes he held in his hand. "He withdrew that bill so that the voters will assume only he can bring it back before the senate when they meet next."

Gathering herself up so that she stood her tallest, she faced both men, a steely sense of resolution in her voice. "Now listen, both of you. Bullock's stab at playing dirty politics is just that—a stab. He well knows that I was in full support of that bill from the very beginning. He also knows that I, along with the Austin Women's Caucus, worked to keep the pressure on him when he was trying to dump it. By then he'd gotten his publicity out of the bill, and all he wanted to do was forget it. We lobbied so hard he didn't dare do anything for fear of looking ridiculous and angering every woman in the state." She nodded, as if she were reaffirming her thoughts. "You two get me the dates that we met with Bullock's assistants and our notes from all of those meetings. I'm going to call a press conference of my own. Ted Bullock's pushed once too often, and now I'm going to have my say. I'm even going to go him one better. The only reason that bill's as good as it is now is because of me. When I'm finished with Ted Bullock he's going to wish he'd never even brought up the issue. He thinks I'm just a docile female and a political novice who'd never dare tell the behind-the-door history of this bill. He probably doesn't even remember that it was me who instigated the pressure to keep the bill alive. Well, I've got surprising news for him."

Earl and Steve were grinning from ear to ear. Earl spoke then. "That man is going to be so sorry he opened all this up he'll wish he'd never even heard of women's rights." He chuckled out loud, and then turned serious once more. "Your statement will have to be worded very carefully. Bullock's going to be on the news at five o'clock this afternoon. I think it would be best if you just laid low until he's gotten his publicity out of this thing. Tomorrow you can address the issues, after you've had time to prepare a statement."

Lindee agreed. She'd found out when she'd had this kind of thing come up before, it was always better to let them happen, ride the waves, and then come back with a reasonable and fair statement. A sudden thought hit her, giving all of this a heightened air of drama, and making her want to laugh out loud. She thought back to what Brooks had said before about politicians.

Just wait, Mr. Griffin, until my press conference tomorrow. I'll show you a thing or two about being able to go the distance.

"The only problem is that you're going to have to stonewall the press until after Bullock's five o'clock showing," Earl was saying. "Stay away, refuse comment, no matter what the question. That's got to be the way you handle the media for the rest of the day."

Easier said than done, Lindee found out as the day wore on. She made her speech at the Chamber of Commerce luncheon, receiving a round of heavy applause at the end. She was interviewed by a woman from the local paper who was interested in finding out what it was like for a woman running for office. They talked about personal things, like how Lindee planned her wardrobe and how she managed to exercise and take care of herself on the road. Lindee found herself liking the interviewer very much, and their meeting ran over by forty-five minutes, putting her behind for the rest of the day.

And wherever she went the reporters hounded her like dogs on a rabbit's trail. Only the special skills of Earl and Steve had kept them away from her. But that night her luck began to run out when she left a dinner party hosted by an old family friend. Plans had already been made to get her outside through the back door. Envisioning a way to end her night before midnight, Lindee followed them as speedily as possible. The hotel was only ten minutes away, and they managed to whisk her away before anyone noticed they were gone.

The curved driveway leading to the hotel was full of cars and people milling around. Only the spotlights from the central spiraling water fountains illuminated the area, and that wasn't enough light to see. Too late Steve and Earl recognized Brooks along with a number of other reporters already clustered near the front door, waiting. With no chance of backing up or turning around, they all agreed there was nothing to do but to pass by the newsmen. They decided to stick closely together.

Lindee braced herself when she stepped out of the car. What

a terrible way to end the day. She turned back to Earl. "Wish me luck," she called.

"Remember, don't let them push you into saying anything."

If he said anything else she didn't hear him. Before she could close the car door, there were four reporters, two men and two women, pushing her back against the car, bursting out questions that couldn't be understood for all the noise they were making as they all shouted into her ear at once.

Four camera lights were turned on just when she'd managed to make her way a few feet closer to the hotel entrance. The terrible glare was blinding. Unwilling to slow down, she pursued her escape, going in the general direction of safety. The only thing she would say in response to the barrage of questions that were being tossed at her was "No comment." Her words had no effect. When she heard Brooks's voice shout over all the others she turned her head but kept going.

"When are you going to have a comment, Miss Bradley?" he called.

"Tomorrow. Tomorrow at ten I will entertain all your questions, but until then I have no comment." Breathless, feeling the overwhelming sensation of being trapped, she put out her arm to hold the reporters back. From someplace near she could hear the cascading water from the decorative fountain. She was close to it; she could see the spotlights out of the corner of her eye, and the noise was almost masking the loud words of the horde pursuing her.

"Miss Bradley, one more question," Brooks said.

Somehow he'd managed to weave his way through the others and he was standing directly behind her. She turned then and saw his cameraman holding the television camera poised for a close-up shot.

Lifting the corner of his mouth, Brooks said, "Mike, start the camera now. Miss Bradley, is it true what Senator Bullock says about you? Have you ignored the needs of the women of Texas?" Over the tumult created by so many others, Brooks's voice rang out clearly, a challenge that would make any candidate want to answer.

Lindee looked at him, cutting her eyes across his face with a reaction that was worth ten thousand words. She opened her mouth to say something. She couldn't let his comments go by without an answer. In a sudden movement that caught her jangled nerves off guard, Brooks stepped forward and at the same time thrust his microphone right up to her face.

Defensively she stepped back, and when he followed suit she stepped back again. She heard Earl's warning shout, but it came a fraction of a second too late.

Lindee felt the backs of her legs connect with an object that had no give, and without another conscious thought she felt herself falling backward. Then she had the sensation of water, and realized she was sopping wet. She'd stepped back to get away from Brooks, and blinded by the lights, she'd managed to fall into the splashing fountain that she'd noticed earlier.

Thousands of thoughts jammed her brain then. She couldn't separate them, but instinct told her that she must look a sight, sitting in the middle of a foot of water with a shower falling down around her. Vaguely she heard the roar of laughter that came from those people staring down at her, but she still was in shock. The camera lights were focused on her and she knew every television, every newspaper in the state would have a picture of the candidate sprawled unceremoniously in the middle of a fountain the next day.

From somewhere Brooks shot out a hand, the first one to get to her, to offer help. Yet his face was distorted with his laughter, and she could see his body shake with the intensity of it.

She reached out her own wet hand to his, barely letting her fingertips graze his. He stepped on the rock ledge of the fountain, the same short ledge she'd stumbled over, and extended his hand, stretching his body out to her, trying to maintain his own balance. She could still hear the laughter and see the effect it was having on Brooks. His body still shook with mirth.

Waiting until he'd reached as far as possible, Lindee lifted her hips and her right leg in a move that ended with perfection. With a twist of her right foot she crooked it up and caught the back of his leg and jerked her own leg back with all her might. Watching him fall down next to her gave her the most perverse of delights. Laughter echoed along the water's surface, but this time it was her own.

She smiled a bedraggled but triumphant smile and then broke into gales of laughter all over again when she saw the look of utter surprise on his face. Earl stepped into the water then and rescued her, throwing his sport jacket around her shoulders and ushering her through the reporters, who now let her pass without interference.

Lindee took a second to look back at the fountain. Brooks was out of the water, sopping wet, his hair glistening in the reflected light, his clothing stuck to the very masculine frame of his body. He looked magnificent, despite what she'd done to him, and damn it all, the man was smiling. Even worse, if she didn't know better, she could have sworn he winked at her.

A little over an hour and a half later, after a soothing hot shower, a phone call from her mother, and a hurried conference with Earl, it seemed no wonder that sleep wouldn't come Lindee's way. She told herself she'd recovered from the water fountain incident, but the mere thought of it being on television made her feel sick with the flush of embarrassment. She blamed Brooks for all of it. If he hadn't been so persistent things never would have progressed as they did. And all those dark thoughts churning through her mind kept her from sleeping, despite her need for rest.

Perched on the edge of the bed, Lindee sat silently studying the curves and lines of her fingers. How was it possible that her life had become so vastly complicated in so short a time, and all because of one man? He intended to use her. Of that much she was certain. From the way he'd acted when they'd been alone, she suspected he intended even more than she'd first thought. He was out to help Ted Bullock win, and he was doing an excellent job of undermining her image. If he'd had a hatchet and she were a block of wood he couldn't do a better job of chipping away at her. He hadn't missed a trick.

Wide awake, tired of fighting herself, Lindee got up from the bed and dug into the bottom of her smallest suitcase until she found her bikini. She'd been wet once already tonight, and a nice peaceful soak in the hotel's hot tub might be the perfect solution to her insomnia, she thought as she wrapped her robe tightly around her body.

Feeling a little apprehensive about the lateness of the hour, she walked quietly across the portico to the enclosed hot tub area. It was pitch dark outside, and the cool air hit her face in a most refreshing way. Now if she could only loosen up, she said to herself.

When she stepped inside and closed the door behind her it was so still and quiet that she felt goosebumps dance along her flesh. The hot tub was built in the middle of a large room. Around its edges a few tables and scattered chairs sat empty. Over in a far, dark corner was a bar, and on a shelf above it was a stereo system. Lindee turned on soft music, and wishing for a glass of chilled Chablis, she took off her robe and shoes, then daintily stepped into the warm bubbling water. It didn't take long for her body to respond to the relaxing pull of the water, and she sat, leaned back against the tub's edge, and closed her eyes.

It seemed as if only moments had passed when she heard a noise at the door. She let out a groan. Brooks strode purposefully across the small enclosure.

"What are you doing here?"

"It's all part of the package, isn't it? Room, free access to the swimming pool and hot tub. The swimming pool's a little too chilly for me, but the hot tub sounded like a good idea."

He threw off his robe and stood still for the briefest of moments, staring down at her. The look in his eyes warned her to be cautious, and she told herself not to look at the way his skin-hugging bathing suit molded itself to his narrow hips, stopping just at the beginning of his muscular thighs. She'd never seen him out of a business suit. It was amazing how much clothes covered up.

Everything about the place became softly still. She could feel his eyes travel along the outline of her bikini, and she lowered her body ever so slightly back into the bubbling water. Tiny clouds of vapor rose up all around her, sending a deceptively relaxed sensation spreading through her body. She'd been in the hot tub just long enough for her limbs to feel light, and for the first time in days her head was free of the tension that stalked her. And now Brooks was here with her.

He watched her sitting there, looking lost and strangely vulnerable. She was tired, he knew that much, and he felt a strong urge to protect this woman. As capable as she was in her own right, he wanted to defend her. He knew she blamed him for what had happened earlier in the evening. He remembered the look she'd given him. That fiery look alone had been enough to precede all hell breaking loose, and yet he admired her for what she'd done next. Pulling him in with her was a stroke of genius as well as plain good fun. Now the media could play up her good sense of humor. Of course, she wasn't looking at it that way, not now.

Forcing herself to action, Lindee murmured, "I was just about to get out. I've been in far too long." Her legs carried her through the warm water in slow motion, and as she started up the steps she reminded herself to keep her eyes lowered and concentrate on the slick steps. The less conversation she had with Brooks, the less conflict they'd stir up between them.

He passed her, saying, "Wait a minute. You're not going anywhere, Lindee."

His fingers brushed against her arm, burning like fire on her skin, and she kept walking forward until she'd reached the second step. Now there was a sense of urgency added to her journey. She definitely didn't want to be here alone with Brooks. She was too happy to see him, and her mind was sending out crazed messages.

"Not so fast." He reached up and pulled her back with him

down into the steamy tub of bubbling water. His arms were forceful and strong, yet she told herself she could pull away from him if she had to. Still, he carried her down with him.

For a moment she forgot how much she wanted to get away from the willful man who sat before her. He was, without a doubt, strikingly handsome. But her critical eye insisted that his jaw was a little too square, his eyes a shade too dark with those thick lashes and heavy brows that made him look as if he had some secret that he kept from the world. And if that observation weren't critical enough, she had to wonder how he managed to maintain his physique with the life he must lead. Any semicelebrity television newsman surely didn't have time for regular meals or steady exercise. Surprisingly fit, his look defied her biased opinions. In competition with her thoughts a memory emerged and filled her senses. He looked just like he had in her dream.

"What do you want? Don't you think there's been enough between us today?" she sputtered, suddenly aware of the myriad of impulses that were awakening, partly in response to the memory of her dream, partially in response to the physical presence of this man.

"Well, now that you brought it up, how about giving me an apology. You got me all wet." He smiled.

"Me? Are you kidding? You're the one who caused it all, you know!" She couldn't control the quiver in her voice.

"I thought you'd see it that way." Slowly, ignoring her words, he brought his lips down upon hers, demanding a response. His tongue broke through her parted lips in deliberate arousal to plunge deeper and deeper in tense investigation, sending a warm stirring rippling through her body. Then, as swiftly as he'd claimed her, he pulled his lips away.

As badly as she hated to admit it, this impetuous man made her want to stay right where she was and let the night ride on. One kiss had awakened an intoxicating sensation deep within her, even as she tried to tell herself it was from exhaustion rather than desire. She couldn't even maintain her anger. With a fierce shake of her head, she admonished herself to leave before anything else happened between the two of them. She would only be hurting herself if she stayed.

"Is this part of your investigative reporting? Am I going to be a special feature on that news program of yours tomorrow, or what? I mean, you've got to be desperate to step into a hot tub with the candidate, don't you think? But they say you always did like to get an unusual slant for your television viewers."

He answered her with a short laugh. "Oh, I don't know—I hadn't planned on stepping into that water fountain either." He laughed again. "Do you see any cameras? I'm off the job right now, and I'm here to concentrate on entertaining myself . . . us. I'm not even going to ask you to give me any advance information about that press conference of yours." The way his eyes stared straight through her made her feel very vulnerable and exposed.

"Well, I think you'd better plan on entertaining yourself. I'm getting out," she said with a defiant toss of her head.

"Why?" His question stopped her forward motion. Its directness didn't surprise her, but the vague hint of tenderness did.

"Why? Are you serious? I don't intend to be around you any more than I have to . . . for a couple of reasons. Surely you realize that if we're seen together there could be a lot of gossip stirred up in this campaign. I've thought a lot about it, especially after yesterday morning. I'm not willing to take the chance. I wouldn't think you would be, either. That wouldn't be good for your career."

She pulled her eyes away from his and started out of the tub once more. Feeling the tension of her own words edge up through her neck and shoulders, she knew she wouldn't be able to sleep anytime soon.

Dammit, Lindee thought. Why was it that he was able to instill this kind of response in her? He was infuriating, impetuous, and much too sure of himself. And most importantly, there was no way she could trust him. But her heartbeat was so loud that she could feel it pulsing through the veins in her temples.

He interrupted her thoughts. "Don't give me any of that stuff. An excuse, that's all you're looking for."

His curt manner made it easy for her to say what was on her mind. "Look, Brooks, I'm not some starry-eyed romantic looking for excitement with the first handsome stranger that comes my way. I told you once I don't need this. I'm perfectly agreeable to doing interviews with you, and to have you along on my campaign, even though I know you don't think I can win. Now, ever since you came along I've been made to look as foolish as any woman could be. Don't, please, don't assume I'm just another fool waiting to succumb to your charms."

He stood then, his hand reaching out to clamp her chin in a viselike grip. Angrily he lashed at her with his words. "For a woman running for such a responsible position I'd think you were smarter than that. I'm here because I want to be with you—not in public—alone, the two of us. What's the matter with you, Lindee? Can't you handle that?"

"Handle that . . . Oh," she cried. "You're even worse than I thought. All you can think of is your own interests—nothing else."

"And what's wrong with that?" he began to shout back. "Look, it's after five o'clock. We're all through for the day. You're not the candidate now and I'm not the reporter. We're two people having fun." His voice was raised, but he was concentrating more on the way her hair looked, as if it had its own magical set of lights as it gleamed a thousand shades in the reflected water's light. "Well, I'm having fun anyway, while you're keeping yourself busy making up silly excuses for keeping me away from you."

"You . . ." she started to say, suddenly aware that he'd reached up to run his fingers through her long hair. "You don't care anything about what my being seen here with you could do to me, do you? You don't care that this could cost me the election. Let go of me," she hissed, afraid she'd cry if she didn't get away in the next few moments. She needed time to sift through what was happening to her. Her emotions were running rampant. She wanted to bolt away, she wanted to stay, she wanted . . . she didn't know what she wanted right now.

Abruptly his tone shifted lower and he let go of her chin, only to take her hand up into his. "Has anyone ever told you that you don't look the part of a candidate for one of the most conservative offices in the state?" He was studying her carefully, aware of the tension in her body, trying to figure out how he could convince her to stay. "For the life of me I can't figure out if you're just unbelievably crazy or maybe naively gutsy enough to be taking this chance. Just look at you."

His eyes roamed up and down her body in a swift, hard analysis that told her nothing of what he was thinking. After a few seconds his eyes came to rest on her face.

"You're too pretty for one thing. Not beautiful, maybe, but striking as hell." He grinned, wondering if she'd be angry at him, but she didn't change her expression. "Besides that, you look too . . . I don't know . . . young, innocent . . . maybe it's that you don't look tough enough. And then there's the fact that you don't smile enough." While he had her attention focused on his words he gently pulled her hand, but she refused to budge, and so they stood where they were. "God knows every politician has to go to bed smiling and get up every morning with another huge smile plastered across his face. That's all part of the game of politics. And if that's not enough against you there's the fact that you're too damned honest. Honesty spells doom in this business. Believe me, I've seen it all too often."

"Listen," she said in a voice full of exasperation. "I'd like to know what it is with you. Are you the expert on politial candidates or something? This is the third time you've tried to tell me about my own business. Besides, who asked for your opinions?" She was disgusted with the way he could maneuver and twist his words to focus her attention on one thing and then in a flash change the subject to something entirely different. She never knew exactly how to deal with him.

"Okay." He sighed and dropped his hand. "You don't want

the truth. We'll talk about something else. What's a fascinating woman like you doing in a place like this?"

His second attempt at teasing irritated her even more. She hated herself for the way she was letting her mind respond to him. She wasn't usually this angry or irrational, and telling herself to stop didn't seem to help. "Where do you think I should be?" she retorted. "Home baking chocolate chip cookies for two kids and a domineering husband?"

"Thank heavens, no," he roared. "No."

Involuntarily she smiled in response to his outburst. He had some of the most disarming qualities she'd ever seen. Fascinating.

He closed his eyes moodily; his voice faded lower and lower. "No, Lindee, not in some man's kitchen. I see you in some man's bed being pampered and made beautiful love to." He waited for a protest. "That's where I see you."

"Look, I'm not at all interested in the way this conversation's going," she stated flatly, all the time hoping her eyes wouldn't give away her true thoughts.

"I didn't figure you would be. You've already demonstrated how much you want to keep your distance from me. But . . ." he said, before abruptly sitting down and pulling her back into the water with a decided splash.

Her mind was full of a thousand slivered images as she wondered why this was happening to her right now. This wasn't the time. Yet over and over again she was reminded of the aura of this man as he pressed his wet body boldly against hers so that they were bound together.

"I know what's right, Lindee," he murmured, and his breath felt warm against the tender skin of her cheek. "We're right, you and I."

He bent to kiss her, his mouth hungry with excitement. The air was thick with the anticipation that hung between them. And when his lips met hers Lindee felt all her senses come alive and the soothing sensation of the water lapping against her legs made her acknowledge the sensuality of the moment. Playfully he moved his mouth across the surface of her lips, testing, analyzing her response.

"Brooks," she murmured, pushing against his chest with a touch much lighter than she'd intended. "This is ridiculous. We can't. Haven't you heard anything I've said to you?"

He looked at her then, and waited, dropping his arms free of her. But if she'd thought she'd turn away she was wrong. Her feet refused to move despite the intent of her words. She told herself that this was the most impossible situation she could have ever thought to find herself in, but her emotions fought for control. There was something so strong, so compelling about Brooks Griffin that she remained still, knowing as she did so that it was possibly the worst mistake of her life.

His mind and body converged in mutual need as he felt a tremor twist through him. He wanted to shout out to her, force her to give up this pretense she insisted upon. He knew as certainly as he knew night followed day that she held herself back, resisted him, while underneath it all her blood pounded as hotly as his.

As if he knew he was being given a chance he spoke up, voice smooth as velvet, spellbinding. "You're fighting the inevitable, Lindee. You're not a kid, and I'm not either. You can't deny that you feel it too. I can tell." Then he brought his lips down gently along the curve of her ear and waited for her response.

"It's not so," she lied.

His lips made a tender trail from her ear to the corners of her eyes, and she knew that it was now or never. No woman in her right mind would continue letting a man embrace her like this if she had no interest in him.

"No more talking."

But she refused to be silent. "We can't, Brooks. Don't you see I can't take the chance of being perceived as some footloose woman who has affairs with the men she meets along the campaign trail?"

Mockingly he taunted her, letting his words fall around her like some seductive cocoon. "Affairs? I was merely going to kiss you." He pressed full lips against the top of her forehead, knowing that he wasn't telling the complete truth, but afraid that if he let her see how much he wanted her, he'd frighten her away. "I had no idea you had anything more than that in mind." Then he laughed, a quiet but hearty laugh, caught up in his own sense of pleasure. "Nobody's going to know a thing."

"Is this what you've been after all along?" she asked breathlessly. She watched the way his mouth curved into a lazy half smile, so blatantly suggestive.

"What do you think?" he murmured huskily, barely able to speak. His body was on the verge of exploding with pent-up desire.

Never again, she vowed silently, would she ever question the sanity of skydivers or fearless mountain climbers or even fire-eaters. The hypnotic thrill of living dangerously was overwhelming. She was caught up in a frightening, exciting, adventurous trance so compelling that it made her want to smile herself. In all her life she'd never once felt this way.

"If you only knew what you do to me, Lindee." He brushed his lips against the soft shell of her ear.

The feelings that raced through her at his touch threatened to shatter her into a thousand pieces. She knew that this was wrong . . . crazy . . . wild . . . destructive . . . all those powerful words and more raced through her mind.

Before she could voice her protest he stopped her with his mouth. He ran his hand up her wet back and pressed her to him with a strength she hadn't known he had, and despite herself she let down her defenses and opened her mouth to the fiery caress of his tongue.

Time washed away from them as they both reacted to the here and now. Responding to the passion of his movements, she brought her arms around his neck and let her lips meet his as her emotions rose to the surface and took control. The overwhelming thrill of the sensations that were rocketing through her body were new, unlike any she'd ever experienced. Never had she even dreamed of the instinctive responses her flesh could make as a violent trembling invaded her body, stirring sleeping passions to wakefulness, and she was powerless to stop herself.

The air hung thick and misty, soft music echoed through the room, and as he brought her nearer she stared in open fascination at the way tiny bubbles of water had caught and remained imprisoned in the tightly curled hairs on his chest. Only a few managed to escape, sending bold rivulets of water running down his chest to places unknown.

And when he brought her onto his lap in the bubbling water she was pliant to the touch, unwilling to disturb the erotic sensations that throbbed deep inside her body. Now she was warm in the water, feeling as if she could float away forever in this languid pool if she could only maintain the way she felt forever. She never wanted this to stop, she told herself as his lips vibrated against the soft skin of her neck and beyond in a slow agonizing path downward to that warm shadowy valley between her breasts.

With one deft movement he reached behind her, unfastened the strap of her bathing suit, and pushed it out of his way and into the bubbling water, while all the time his lips traced gentle unhurried patterns along every line where the bikini top had been. Her senses were alive and in control now, brushing away all rational thought.

She ran her fingers through his thick hair, letting them come to rest at the base of his neck, memorizing the feel of his skin, absorbing the masculine scent of him, listening for the beat of his heart.

She would never have heard it, but abruptly Brooks held her still. A noise sounded outside.

"Hey, Brooks, I hate to disturb you, but the big boss is waiting on the line. He says he needs to talk to you right away." Mike, the cameraman assigned to Brooks, knocked at the door. "He says it's important. They've switched the call to the phone right outside. You can take it by the pool."

With a quick glance at Lindee's face Brooks said, "There is

no justice." His teeth were clenched. "Okay, I'll be right there," he yelled out.

She wouldn't look at him until he tilted her chin in his direction. "I'll be right back," he sighed, caressing her arms with his own powerful hands. "Don't you move. Hear?"

Like an obedient servant she stayed where she was, watching as he quickly stepped out of the pool and hurriedly dried himself off. He picked up his robe and threw it around his broad shoulders before looking at her once more.

"I mean it. Don't move."

She watched the back of him until he was out of sight. The instant he disappeared from view all the confusion and doubts she'd suppressed returned with a mighty rage. Now was the time to leave.

That had been a close call, too close. Why Mike hadn't opened the door and stepped inside she'd never know, but whatever his reason, it was almost as if he had. He'd had the power, with one gentle twist of the doorknob, to have ended her career. There she'd been, locked in an intimate embrace with Brooks, the top to her bathing suit lying at the bottom of the hot tub, long forgotten. What just happened was absolute proof that her reasons to stay away from Brooks were correct. Being with him was a capricious act that could never be justified.

She'd lost her senses when Brooks had taken her in his powerful arms. And with each second she'd let herself stay there with him, her self-control had disappeared. Not only had she closed her mind to the possibilities of someone coming inside, she'd never even considered that there could have been someone outside when she got ready to leave. The absurdity of what she'd done rushed over her with a vengeance. All she wanted to do was get out of there fast.

Feeling weak and off balance, she grabbed the top to her bathing suit and put it on as quickly as her trembling fingers would allow. She stepped out of the tub, gathered up her robe, and left, carefully looking over her shoulder as she made her way back to her lonely hotel room.

As she walked she talked to herself. What she'd just done was unbelievable—a tempestuous mistake from beginning to end. She should have left the instant he entered the room, and to have let him touch her like that—well, it made absolutely no sense.

Yet that was only part of what she'd felt. Mostly she felt changed—disappointed by the interruption. What she'd wanted was to be able for just a moment to feel a sense of togetherness with him, and instead she felt dreadfully incomplete.

He was like a sorcerer, bringing all sorts of feelings to life. Brooks had laughed and teased away all her protests tonight, refusing to give any credibility to what she'd been attempting to tell him. If he was unwilling to take her election seriously, naturally it would follow that he'd not bother to consider the consequences of their being together—or even worse, maybe that was all part of the plan. . . .

But dwelling on the negative wasn't what she wanted right now, not after what she'd just experienced. First one thought struck her and then another came closely behind—mixing, twirling around—like raindrops in a summer storm. Oh God, she felt like a rag doll about to be torn helplessly in two.

Huge tears splashed down her cheeks, blinding her as she walked. Was there no answer? She didn't know what to think except that she'd discovered feelings inside herself that she'd never known existed, and good or bad, they were there now—alive—resting—quietly waiting.

CHAPTER FOUR

The loud knock on the door of her hotel suite a few minutes later should have come as no surprise, but it created such an overwhelming, jangling surge of excitement that she jumped up from the chair where she'd been sitting, trying to force herself to look through her notes for the next day. Attempting to calm herself, she pulled her robe tightly around her and retied the belt before answering, one part of her hoping beyond hope that it would be him, another part telling her heart to be silent.

"Who is it?" she asked through the solid wood.

"If I didn't know better, I'd think you were serious," Brooks's voice boomed out in the thin night air. "Open this door."

"Brooks, please." She yielded, unchaining the latch, so afraid he might be heard by someone else. "Keep your voice down."

"What is it with you?" His eyes sparkled with a light that refused to be dimmed, and he brushed his fingers through his hair in absentminded distraction. "Why did you leave just now? I told you I'd be right back. I got rid of the man on the telephone as quickly as I could."

She loved the way he looked, his damp hair curling in ringlets, his eyes a little confused, off guard. A different man, one not quite so sure of himself, bordering on the irresistible in what seemed to be an emerging vulnerability. A warning bell sounded in her ears. She couldn't let this man get to her. She'd nearly blown it once tonight. Not again.

"Brooks, you've got to leave." Tightly gripping her robe to her with one hand, she kept the door partially closed with the other, effectively barring his entrance. "Don't you realize what nearly happened back there? We could have been caught. . . . Oh, Brooks." She slowly shook her head. Her voice softened when she looked up at him, seeing the doubt flicker across his eyes. He didn't know what she was talking about. "Mike could have opened that door and found us there so easily. Anyone could have come in or even been sitting outside by the pool and seen us come out."

"But they didn't," he charged. "Mike didn't open that damned door and nobody was out by the pool. Furthermore, nobody saw me come up here either."

Sadly she shook her head again, bewildered that he could remain so totally unconvinced. "But they could have. I can just see it all now. The headlines would read 'Legislative Candidate Seen Topless in Tub with Newsman.' Oh, that would make wonderful copy." A grimace crossed her face when she let her imagination toy with the idea.

"If your political career doesn't work out, you might have a chance with *The National Enquirer*," he teased. "Lindee, let me in." He lightly pushed on the door, never taking his eyes away from hers. "Nobody saw me come here. I've already told you that, and besides, what possible difference can it make? We happen to be two private people tonight. There are no reporters now."

Steadfastly holding the door, she felt anger rise up to replace the fleeting sadness she'd experienced at not being able to make him understand. "You still don't understand, Brooks. This is a tremendous risk I'm taking, even standing here right now with you. We're not private people, you and I, no matter what time of the day or night it happens to be. We're very much in the public eye."

"Okay, okay. I hear what you're saying, but that's a philosophical issue, Lindee. One that you and I obviously seem to be in disagreement over." His face changed then, his features softening ever so slightly. When he spoke he was full of that disarming charm she'd come to know, and there was a trace of husky sensuality pulsating just below the surface of his next words. "We can't discuss this through the door. Let me in and we'll talk it out." Then, not waiting, rubbing at his robed arms like they were chilled, he pushed his way inside, giving her a gentle smile as he entered.

"For five minutes and then that's it," she said, flinging caution to the winds as she moved aside, letting him pass her, and closed the door. But suddenly she froze. The very air of the room had changed, filled now with the chemistry that crackled between them. Willingly she'd let him in, and now there was no backing down. He was here and there was a question to be answered between them. They both waited for the answer.

"You're driving me mad," he told her gravely, his eyes suddenly filled with desire. He reached out for her. "I want you, Lindee, and you want me."

Oh, no. Why had she done this? She berated herself. Why had she let this man inside when she knew what kind of power he held? "No, Brooks. Don't start that," she insisted, struggling against the messages her body was sending out while he stood so near her. They were wild, screeching, crazed messages. It seemed suddenly every part of her was aflame. She felt a tingling sensation steal all along her legs, her hands and arms were on fire, and even her ears burned with this feeling, as her body grew frantic, irately demanding to be given in to like some spoiled, petulant child. Willing herself to speak, she said, "If you want to talk, fine. If not, you'd better leave. Your time's running out even as we stand here."

"Just keep talking. Say anything you wish." He watched her face fill with new confusion even as he reached over and brought her to him, letting his mouth hover over her lips for the briefest instant, then kissing her before she could say anything more.

Their lips met, and once more he surprised her with the absorbing, all-consuming way his lips spoke to hers. His kiss brought back all the passion, aroused all the desire they'd earlier shared. It was an attempt to reunite them once more, and with a sigh that touched both of them Lindee felt her resistance ebb away from her as she let her tongue meet his in restless exploration. A trembling seized her when he began to run his hand down along her back before it came to rest along the curve of her hip.

"Now," he said. "Tell me you don't want me. Tell me that and I'll leave, but don't tell me a lie, Lindee."

There was nothing brash in the way he spoke. It was, instead, as though he was waiting for her to acknowledge what there was between them. His eyes spoke of passion, but there was truth there also.

Lifting her face to his, she tilted her head back and studied every line of his face, taking in the faint touches of gray that grew at his temples, noticing the fullness of his lips and the distance between his eyes. I'm going to regret this, she thought, and heard an inner voice pleading with her to stop. Unconsciously she reached up to trace a line from the base of his ear down to where the collar of his robe touched his neck.

Then she heard a far-off voice and with a start realized it was her own. "I want you, Brooks. Much more than I knew."

Deep inside her, in a concealed area she hadn't even known existed, somewhere just below the pit of her stomach, a new, very real sensation had awakened tonight. Brought to life by Brooks's caress, this feeling that had taken control so easily, so suddenly, was not to be refused. Each time her mind said no, this primeval response pulsed through her, breaking waves of fresh sensations into full wakefulness, shutting out all other thoughts as effectively as if she were turning off a light.

She'd have this man and consequences be damned. As long as she'd lived she'd never once been challenged by her body before, and all her senses screamed out for the man standing before her.

This wasn't the time for thinking. It couldn't be. . . . Her mind was moving into the game itself, reveling in a insatiable desire that had grabbed her, refusing to let go, demanding fulfillment.

"Oh, Lindee," he groaned softly, picking her up into his arms. He felt a freedom that he'd never known, an excitement that couldn't be contained, and he dismissed all other thoughts from his mind. He wanted this woman and he wouldn't be denied. She was too much; a gift, a spell, a spark of magic that he longed to possess if only for a moment. And when he reverently laid her across the bed he stood for a long time, his eyes locked with hers, before he slowly began to undress.

She caught her breath as she watched him remove his robe with a slight tug on the belt and a quick shrug of his broad shoulders. Then she left the bed and stood next to him, not knowing what it was she wanted to do. But she followed her instincts as she reached over and crooked her thumbs into the damp waistband of his bathing suit. She noticed the shudder that ran through him and she lifted her lips to give him a fleeting kiss before she helped free him of the imposing clothing. Longing to run her fingers along every part of his muscular body, Lindee smiled up at him, responding with total pleasure to the desire his body could not hide.

But Brooks had his own thoughts, and he gathered her into his arms and brushed her thick mane of hair back away from her neck before he bent to kiss the proud curve of her chin and then the tender shell of her ear. How was it that a woman who gave to the public eye the illusion of composure and total sophistication could keep hidden this beautiful fiery existence? he wondered. But he'd felt it all along, he realized. Felt it and longed to discover for himself the straightforward burst of passion that shimmered just below the surface of Lindee Bradley.

He moved back and began a torturously slow removal of her robe, letting his hands stop along the way to caress her softly curved shoulders, her upper arm, and then, when she thought he'd drop the robe to the floor, he brought it up around her arm and caught both her breasts into the fabric of the soft cloth, holding her captive to the heated kisses he sent cascading along each of her breasts until she knew she might scream with the sheer pleasure of it all. She moaned aloud as he brought his teeth together to gently graze her rigid nipples.

She flung back her head and pressed herself against his virile form, longing for release and at the same time knowing she wanted this to go on forever. All Lindee could feel were the messages of her body crazed with desire. No words were needed, no conscious thoughts were wanted here. She was caught up in a passion that suddenly knew no bounds, and she would have given up everything for the pleasures of the moment.

Brooks removed her robe and flung it to the floor. "Let me look at you," he demanded in a tone that was filled with an urgent curiosity, and while she hated to release him she understood his desire and stepped away from him.

What he saw was not exactly what he'd envisioned. It was far better. Without the clothes that masked her body like velvet over precious jewels Brooks saw the perfection of the woman she was. Unable to resist, mad to touch her, he ran his fingers along the curve of her waist and around each breast, stopping so often that she thought he might soon know her flesh better than she did. Unwilling to stop, he let his fingers run along her stomach, acknowledging once with his eyes the delighted shiver of goosebumps she was unable to control, and then he plunged farther, tracing a line along her firm thighs and hips, then back to the most secret part of her where he let his hand stay until she begged him to release her.

And then it was her turn as she followed suit, letting her fingers run wild along his skin in aching ecstasy, letting herself linger over unfamiliar delights, exploring, yet knowing it would take a very long time to discover all that this man had to give.

"Lindee," he moaned, and pulled her to him, gently probing her tender flesh, willing himself to hold off as long as he could so that she could feel the spell as much as he did. But he was on the verge of being dangerously out of control, and he pulled her to him on the bed. When their eyes locked in mutual desire he took her in a maddening ecstasy that locked them together in a bursting flash of tempestuous climax. With each move he made she responded, moving her hips in an age-old pattern that matched his as if they'd been made for each other, and indeed the bewildered joy she felt made her think perhaps they had.

But—she told herself—only in another world, another place, another time.

Much later, after he'd gone and taken with him all physical reminders of their union, she lay there in the cool, still silence feeling the icy waves of panic slam against her naked body with such force she found she was holding her breath. First one burning tear and then another had forged a path along her cheeks, followed by an onslaught that soon had her pillow drenched.

Why such agony, and why did it have to follow the beautiful glow of rapture so quickly that they'd almost collided? "Life isn't fair," she cried out in the lonely room. She'd found something good, something beautiful, something she needed. Why, oh, why did she have to give it up? Her sobs tore from her body in great gasping gulps of pain.

Like the coward that she felt she was, she hadn't been able to bring herself to tell him before he'd left, couldn't bear to end the ecstatic spell any sooner than she had to. She'd let herself take pleasure in the afterglow of their lovemaking, responding to the touch of his hands, listened with joy to the lovely words he'd bestowed upon her. And even while she'd allowed herself the luxury of taking pleasure in all that was happening, she knew it could not be.

If—and she prayed to God that the worst wouldn't happen—she were fortunate enough to escape without being found out tonight, if Brooks kept quiet and nobody happened to have seen them together, if all of those ifs worked out, she swore to herself that she would never let this happen again.

And if she were found out and all her life's work came tumbling down upon her, then she'd have to bear the punishment.

She was at fault. Brooks might be doing what he wanted to do, considering it an act of his own free will, or he might even be setting her up by taking advantage of her. She'd know soon enough, but in a way, it hardly mattered. Oh, she thought with a grimace, it mattered to her, certainly, but if what she'd done tonight were discovered she had only one person to blame when all was said and done.

She walked slowly over to the mirror and looked at the reflection there. She was to blame. She alone controlled her life. She'd made her choice and if it turned out to be a disastrous one she'd have to look no farther than her own mirror to discover the guilty party.

She could only look forward now. The past had to be forgotten. In the future, no matter what Brooks might say, no matter how convincingly he presented himself as well as his logic, she would not dare let him control her. And she knew he'd return, wanting her, willing her protests away with a joke and a kiss. But whether he would agree or not, Lindee knew only one thing about the two of them. They could not, under any circumstances, let this happen again.

And as she felt her body recall the miraculous moments that they had shared, Lindee knew that she'd have to stay far away from Brooks. For no matter what her mind told her about his overwhelming ambitions and the danger that the man presented, she'd come alive in his arms, and it made her feel afraid of what she might do again.

A series of faces marched before her as she sat on the edge of the bed, trying to stanch the flow of her own tears. First came Earl's, full of trust and confidence; the strain of the campaign showing in the lines below his eyes. Then her mother's, smiling, full of courage and confidence. Behind their faces were all those people Lindee had asked for support.

She knew she couldn't risk what she'd done tonight again. There was no choice. Trying to banish the faces from her thoughts, she got up and looked at the clock, and then sat back down on the bed again. "Oh, God, how I wish I could hate him," she said, and when there was no answer she said, "But I'd hate myself even more."

Her chin began to tremble, her hands shook ever so slightly, and the tears streamed down her face once again. It wasn't fair. No matter what happened she couldn't win, and she couldn't even begin to think about what she might lose.

CHAPTER FIVE

"Earl, help me out this morning, all right?" Lindee asked the next day. "I know those reporters are going to be hounding me after the press conference, no matter how many facts and details I give them. I'd like to leave as soon as I finish. Maybe Steve could have the car ready and we can go straight from the press conference to the car."

The private dining room of the hotel was empty except for the two of them and one slow-moving waitress. The other staffers had left after a brief meeting prior to Lindee's scheduled news conference in the adjoining room. Through the walls she could hear the sounds of people gathering, waiting for her to speak although it was still a little over ten minutes until she would start. Earl had arranged to have coffee and doughnuts set up for the reporters, a maneuver meant to keep them from following Lindee around as much as anything.

He nodded his agreement. "Consider it as good as done, Lindee. Sometimes I think those people are part bloodhound. They never let up. Brooks has already been knocking at my door, asking where you were. He said he'd seen you late last night and looked for you in your room this morning, but you were gone already." Earl sipped from his coffee cup and began buttering his toast with quick, purposeful strokes of the knife, avoiding the question of where she had been, although the inflection in his voice asked.

"I took an early walk down by Town Lake. I couldn't sleep and the view of the capitol is beautiful from there." She fidgeted with a spoon, turning it over and over on the linen tablecloth. Earl's mention of Brooks's name was like having him appear in the room with her. He hadn't really left her mind since he'd left her bed sometime in the dark hours of the night, but neither had her consuming sense of guilt.

Lindee forced herself to listen to what Earl was saying while her mind raced with all the beautiful memories of the evening she'd shared with Brooks. If she closed her eyes she could still feel where his lips had touched her skin, burning with the thrill of the contact, bringing her to life in his arms. She bit her lip as she recalled how their bodies had come together with a will all their own in an experience that had been so intoxicating she'd almost felt in touch with her own destiny for the briefest of moments. It was a remembrance she never wanted to lose.

But once Brooks left her side she'd not been able to rest. Her body, tired and satiated in the most prodigious way, had relaxed, but her mind had not. And telling herself how wonderful it had been between the two of them was a wasted effort. They had no future together. Twice she'd put herself in compromising situations with Brooks, and twice she'd risked her life's desire for a few stolen moments with him. To allow it to go on would be courting disaster, and Lindee knew she couldn't risk it. Too much was riding on this election.

And if those reasons weren't enough, her mind insisted, she could find plenty more. What about the trust factor? What about Brooks's own schemes and plans? She'd almost driven herself crazy with the most distrustful of ideas. Did he care? Had he actually found something to care about in her? Or was he merely playing out one more ploy to involve her in? Would there be hidden cameras or would he tell someone else about their liaison? She didn't think so, but she'd know soon.

"What do you think?" Earl's voice made its way into her consciousness, jarring her back to the present. What was he talking about? Oh, yes, the best way to handle the challenge that Bullock had issued. Earl had copies of their notes from meetings held in Austin over the women's rights bill, proof of Lindee's affirmative actions.

Lindee sipped at her cold coffee and nodded her head. "I'm convinced that after we tell them about what he's done, Bullock will look just as ridiculous as he should." She smiled then. "Of course, Earl, these reporters are always interested in stirring up something. It makes good copy. Right?" She thought of Brooks.

Earl reached across the table, nearly knocking over the salt shaker that stood in his way. "You're right, my friend. Absolutely right." He gripped her hand tightly. "Don't be nervous. Go out there and knock them dead. Pretend you're an actress about to make her theatrical debut." They both stood. "Break a leg."

He'd seen it, she decided. Or felt it. Earl knew something was wrong, and no matter how much she'd tried to hide it she'd failed. Well, her eyes were a little puffy from crying and her face drawn from lack of sleep. She hoped that was what the reporters would think—that she was tired from the campaign itself. Lindee slipped on her glasses, the ones she used for reading. The pale amber tint in the lenses might help conceal the look in her eyes. She hoped so.

Willing herself to be strong, she straightened her shoulders and took the photocopied papers from Earl's hand. Entering the adjoining room, she felt a hush fall over the gathering, and the reporters stood quietly waiting for her to address them from the center podium. She smiled and began adjusting the microphone. Looking all around the room, taking her time, deliberately calming herself, she smiled more confidently. It was going to be okay. With a swift nod of her head, she signaled her readiness to begin.

Brooks stood to the left of his cameraman, trying to get her attention. He wanted to ask her the all-important question about Bullock. She knew that, he told himself, and yet she was deliberately averting her eyes. Hastily he walked over and sat down with the other reporters. Maybe now she'd acknowledge him.

Warm memories of the night before washed over him as he sat there staring up at her. God, what a woman. Unmindful of how strongly he was reliving their interlude, he grinned, and it was then that she looked over at him.

"Miss Bradley," he said, alert now, ready to zero in on his question.

"I believe the AP reporter is next, Mr. Griffin," she told him calmly, effectively cutting him off.

He saw her tilt that finely cut chin of hers and glance away as if he were just another annoying reporter. She stood at the podium in a bright rust-colored suit made of suede, cut long and lean to catch the observer's eye and hold it on the fine curves of her figure. Her only jewelry was a gold watch and square cut topaz earrings that vied with her eyes for all the light that was on her. She wore her hair pulled back, away from her face, and she seemed unmindful of the tender trails of curling strands that fell next to her ear, gently defying restraint. How he longed to take her away right then and there. He could imagine how his hands might tremble as they took down her hair, letting it fall softly to her shoulders. He wanted to smell its clean, fresh fragrance and hold it to his face.

And then he found himself hearing her answer to Bullock's accusation and he couldn't believe himself. Could he have become so lost in a daydream that he'd totally forgotten where he was? He looked around at the others. Hastily moving to the edge of his chair, he reentered the present.

Lindee was passing out a piece of paper with dates and names on it. She said, "There are enough copies for everybody. On the sheet you will see a series of dates and beside those dates a list of names. Any one of those people may be contacted by you, if you so desire, to substantiate what I have said. They were all witnesses. Ted Bullock's name you will notice is missing. Not once did Mr. Bullock bother to attend any of the meetings about the women's rights bill. I repeat, not one time. We met with two of his key aides and ironed out the wording and the improvements. I'm not sure Mr. Bullock even knew what the final bill said. And so you see, ladies and gentlemen, when Ted Bullock accuses me of not being responsive to women's rights and to his bill, well, I can only say how quickly we forget. In fact, it may be that, despite his apparent lack of interest in his own bill, Mr. Bullock intends to use it as a lever to win this election. I think he demonstrated this when he withdrew the bill from consideration, only to promise that he will bring it before the senate in the next session."

Pausing for a second, she let the reporters talk among themselves. "The transcripts of my meetings concerning the bill will be made available," she continued. "Steve is having them typed up now. If any of you have any doubts remaining about my loyalty to women's rights, I'd be glad to answer your questions now and in my debate with Mr. Bullock."

Brooks stood up. "I have a question, Miss Bradley." Their eyes locked, and then he watched her as she quickly glanced away.

"Yes."

"Why do you think Ted Bullock would have made those accusations, knowing that you could prove him wrong?" His face revealed nothing, his voice remained impassive as he waited for her reply.

With a mocking grin, Lindee gave him her answer. "I believe Mr. Bullock didn't even know that I was the one who organized the group's support. Like I say, he never attended any of the committee meetings. He sent his aides. As it turns out his two aides have since left his employ, and so I can only assume that the senator had what you might call a communication problem."

Two other reporters jumped up, competing for a chance to question her further, while the others laughed among themselves. "Miss Bradley," one of them asked, "do you think this will hurt Mr. Bullock?"

She was ready to leave now, growing impatient, knowing in advance how the questioning could drone on and on. But there was no doubt that she'd scored a victory. "I'm not going to reply to that one. The voters of this district will have to decide."

"Miss Bradley, before you go, one more question." Brooks's voice boomed out across the room as she turned away to leave the podium. "Aren't you breaking a code of sorts? I mean, isn't there sort of an unwritten agreement among you politicians that you don't reveal what goes on between you?"

She fought to hold off her astonishment, once again reminding herself that his reputation was well deserved. Well, she had to admit that he was forcing everything out into the open, all the political intrigue that usually went on. And that was why his reputation as an ace investigative reporter had spread.

A smile broke from her lips. "Oh, I don't know if you could say that, Mr. Griffin. If I'm breaking anything, I'd rather consider it breaking into the truth. If I've stepped on anyone's toes I'm sorry, but the voters need to know the truth. Mudslinging campaigns hold no interest for me. That's why I've come here today to tell you the facts. I'll make no judgments. As I said earlier, the voters will have to do that." She reached out for Earl's hand and stepped quickly away, listening as Steve gave them more information. When she saw Brooks get up and start toward her she turned to Earl. "Where's the car?"

They walked out of the lobby with Steve running to catch up with them. "The car's right outside," he said, passing them by and running on out the door.

Brooks pushed his way through the reporters crowding in behind her. Just as he was near enough to reach out and touch her he watched Earl put his arm around her shoulders and pull her to him.

"Listen, we'll see all of you good people later," Earl called. "Our next stop is San Antonio, where Miss Bradley will address a group of women at three thirty at the Hemisfair Plaza. Tonight we'll be in Houston for a fund-raising dinner, then back to San Antonio for a few days. You're welcome to follow our caravan, but no more questions, please. Now if you can follow all that, great." He laughed and the others joined in. He waved his good-byes and ushered Lindee out the door to the waiting car.

"Lindee, wait. Hey, I want to talk to you," Brooks shouted above the voices of the others who stood outside watching her step into the car. She turned and gave him a nod that could have meant anything.

"You heard the man, Mr. Griffin. No more questions," one of the reporters standing near him snapped.

Before he could control himself enough to muster a reply the car was leaving, followed by three more with Lindee Bradley banners all along their sides. Some of the other reporters were already walking to their own vehicles for the seventy-mile drive to San Antonio.

"Dammit, Lindee. You're not getting away with that," Brooks mumbled angrily, wanting to shout it to the heavens. "Mike, get your buns over here. We're going to beat them to their destination."

As irritated as he was with her shabby treatment of him, Brooks was filled with a renewed touch of admiration. That woman had done it again. Each time he thought he'd figured her out she'd swing another surprise his way, and this one had been a big one. She was full of fire, and Brooks loved it. When she'd said what she had about Ted Bullock it was all he could do to keep from laughing out loud. No other candidate would have dared do that, challenge the old-timer in that way. And yet Lindee had stood up there and in so many words managed to call the man a liar. Better yet, she had proof, documented proof. He shook his head. She became more and more convincing as a candidate as the days wore on. Who could tell what might happen next?

Settled in the car, Lindee took off her shoes and stretched out. It was going to be one hell of a long day, and she knew enough to know that she should grab any relaxation time she could. Steve drove and Earl sat up front, his briefcase open, ready for them to discuss her next speech.

"Guess what," Earl said brightly. "You were wonderful."

"Thanks," she said thoughtfully. *Funny,* she thought, *as bad as I feel I can still concentrate on what I'm doing.* But she hadn't forgotten any of her concerns, and she was relieved that Brooks hadn't made any revelations about their night together. He'd had plenty of opportunity this morning.

"I bet Bullock's going to have a four-star headache when he hears about this." Earl laughed.

"Yes, well, I think Mr. Bullock will be quiet now." Lindee looked out the window and sighed. "For a little while, at least."

"I wonder what Brooks wanted?" Earl looked back over at his shoulder at her, lost in his own thoughts.

"What? What do you mean, Earl?" She sat up in the seat, cautioning herself not to be alarmed.

"Well, this morning he was looking for you. It was awfully early, and then he was calling out to you, trying to talk to you before we got into the car. He wouldn't tell me anything and I can't figure out what he wants, unless it's another interview."

Hold yourself together, she said silently. "I have no idea, Earl, but I can guess that he probably wanted to get advance information from me. Isn't that what all those reporters want?" She prayed Earl would let the conversation drop.

"Ha," he laughed. "You really think a lot of that man, don't you?"

"Oh, yes," she answered, and her words held many meanings.

She leaned her head back against the soft cushioned seat and let the car lull her while she listened to Earl talk. Her mind was full of so many thoughts and images that she couldn't control them. Vivid pictures of the night before kept dancing before her eyes, and she fought to stop them. What happened between herself and Brooks was merely a moment torn from time, a brief escape from reality, a fantasy fulfilled. But it had to be forgotten. She couldn't bear to think of what might have happened to them, still could happen. Now she realized that she'd never be free of the cloud of intimidation, never be able totally to dismiss the night from her mind. At any time Brooks could bring it up, reveal how they'd been together. If it weren't purposeful, he could do so accidentally. He'd already aroused Earl's curiosity. She'd taken a foolhardy chance and it made her angry at herself, at Brooks, at life.

What had nearly happened with Mike was further proof of the impossibly dangerous situation that existed between Lindee and Brooks. Lindee had played with fire and she could have easily been burned. She still could. There was no conceivable way that she could let down her guard ever again. To trust Brooks now would be a crazy thing to do—even crazier than what she'd done last night, and that had been the ultimate in stupidity. Trusting now was simply too dangerous, too frightening a proposition.

The mere thought of having any more to do with him gave her cold chills and made her want to clamp her eyes tightly shut and hold back the world. She was too dreadfully vulnerable right now. Better to hold up her defenses like some strong mantle of honor than to take a chance on perhaps losing everything she'd worked for. And if the night hadn't been so damnably wonderful, and if he'd only leave her alone, she certainly could have held up fine.

By the time they reached San Antonio she found herself concentrating on the campaign once again with only an occasional flash of memory's interference. Before walking into the San Antonio Women's Caucus meeting Lindee turned to look at Earl. "Any particular advice?"

"No, just be yourself. Follow your instincts. You've done a great job so far."

Earl turned out to be right. After Lindee made a short opening statement the questions came hard and fast. But a great many of these women were friends, good friends whom she'd worked with before, and she had nothing but the highest regard for them.

"What are we supposed to do, now that you've given us your side of the issues?" demanded a woman in the front row.

"I think you're going to have to do what you've done all along. Study the issues, the candidates, and then vote your convictions," she replied.

Scattered applause broke out in parts of the room.

"Easily said; not so easy to do," came another voice.

Then an old and trusted friend of Lindee's stood up. "Lindee, I think you know that all of us want to support you. We really do."

Lindee smiled. "Thank you, Belinda. I appreciate that."

"But we're worried," the woman went on. "We want more than anything to get a bill passed that will prove fair to the women of this state. We've all wanted it for a very long time. Thanks to you, Bullock's going to end up with so much attention drawn to him that he'll have to support this thing, support and protect it right down the line. If we vote for him we'll end up with a women's rights bill. It's practically guaranteed."

"I know what you're saying, Belinda, and your point is well made. However, don't count me out. It should go without saying that if I'm elected I'm going to bring the same bill up for a vote. It shouldn't take long, I hope."

Another woman stood. "But as a new senator you might have a hard time getting something like that through right away. Those other senators are not going to be too eager to listen to you, not initially, anyway."

For the next half hour the issue was hotly discussed. It was clear that most of the women were behind her, but at the same time they knew they had Bullock right where they wanted him.

"I'll tell you this last thing, my dear friends. I can't promise you that six months from now you'll have that bill passed. Nobody can, no matter what they say. But I'll guarantee you this. I'll fight for it. I'll give it my best effort, and that's all I can do."

Earl sensed the effect of her last words and promptly rose from his chair. "Well, ladies, thank you all. I think the time has come for the candidate to leave. Her presence is promised elsewhere. Thank you again."

Lindee waved and began to walk away amid a standing ovation and the noise of loud cheers. She'd made her mark with these women. A mutual respect had been created, regardless of the outcome.

* * *

By the time they'd finished with that meeting Lindee was exhausted, and both Steve and Earl knew it, but they were running a tight schedule and so they drove in silence to the airport. It was an hour to Houston and she had to be dressed and ready by six thirty. Then she was to leave and fly home again on the ten o'clock flight.

Four hours and ten minutes later she stood in the ballroom of the Warwick Post Oak Hotel, satisfied with the job she'd done, elated by the many people who'd come to the dinner in her honor.

"We're going to form a receiving line of sorts right down here, Lindee," Earl whispered. "Everyone wants to congratulate you." Absentmindedly he patted her shoulder before leading her down from the podium.

"Lindee, we need to talk," Brooks said, standing at the foot of the steps. He looked at Earl, aware that they weren't alone, but desperate to have just a moment with her. The way she had behaved so far, they might never have shared the beautiful moments together that he remembered so vividly. Here he was, totally immobilized by his fascination for her, and she stood there looking at him as if she didn't know him.

"Well, this is hardly the place, and what's more, there's no time," she replied hastily. "All interviews are scheduled for after the reception." She couldn't bring herself to look at him.

The television cameras were already strategically placed, someone had the crowd moving to one side, and Lindee began to shake outthrust hands before she had taken two steps forward. Her hands were cold and she fought to keep her expression spontaneous. Out of the corner of her eye she saw Brooks walk slowly away, and she wanted to run to him, but she held herself back.

Earl had gathered everyone of those who'd come to the elegant five-hundred-dollar-a-plate dinner in an area near the bar, where they waited to have a word with Lindee while sipping perfectly chilled champagne.

"Lindee, you remember Tom Farris, don't you?" Earl asked, casually placing her hand into that of the older gentleman who stood peering down at her.

She shook the bald man's hand, trying not to think about the ache that was being reawakened in her tender fingers after three months of campaigning. She gave him an encouraging smile. "Of course. How are you, Mr. Farris, and how's everything in Kendall County?"

She saw Earl move to her side, ready to help urge those people along who might take up too much of the candidate's time. Everybody wanted to shake hands, do something to share in the making of a famous personality, and politics was the easiest way Texas had for doing it. It was strange, but just as true about all of these people, even though most of them could buy and sell her family ten times over.

"And, Lindee, look who's come all the way from Abilene to see you tonight, P.J. and Eileen." Earl's cheeks were bright with exertion.

Now Lindee gave all her attention to the man and his wife standing before her. P. J. Johnson was the richest oilman in all of Texas, and as eccentric as he was, Lindee took a special delight in knowing he was her friend. Like most of the people in the room, P.J. wouldn't be able to vote for her. He wasn't a resident of her district, but he had widespread influence, something her staff insisted she needed in these final days of the campaign.

His wife kissed Lindee's cheek, leaving a bold mark of crimson just below her left cheekbone. "Oh, Lindee, we're so proud of you. So is everybody we talk to about you, honey. I think you're going to win." The bejeweled woman patted her husband's rotund stomach to get his attention. "P.J. does too. Don't you, P.J.?"

His voice was like a frog's croak when he spoke. "Now, Lindee, you wouldn't want me to tell you anything but the truth, would you?"

The way he said it, Lindee knew she didn't want to hear what was coming next. A hint of resignation was in every word he'd already spoken. A cautious smile flashed across her face. She'd rather hear the truth from him than some others she could name. P.J. had always cared about her; he wouldn't fail her now. "No, I wouldn't, P.J. What is it?"

"You can't win, honey." He kissed her on the cheek before standing back away from her and staring directly into her eyes with his own grave ones. "There ain't no way Ted Bullock's going to let you beat him. He's a tough old codger, and he knows dirty tricks you haven't dreamed of even in a nightmare."

"Oh, P.J., what an awful thing to say to little Lindee. Really," his wife interrupted. Reaching out for Lindee's hand, the woman shook her head disgustedly. "He can be such a crotchety old thing."

Not backing off for a second, P. J. Johnson continued. "Well, Lindee wanted the truth. Maybe next time, but not this election. That's all I'm saying." He glared at his wife before eyeing Lindee speculatively. "You're too naive and inexperienced for this man and there ain't no way he's going to let you beat him. Just make a good showing this time, and let's wait for him to retire. Then you can do it next time around. If you don't believe me, ask that news fella over there. He's supposed to be the smartest guy around when it comes to politics. Ask him and see if he doesn't agree with me."

Not wanting to, but unable to resist the impulse, Lindee looked over at where Brooks was standing, conferring with his cameraman. His head was bent and she let her eyes linger on the muscular curve of his neck, and although she tried to still the flare of excitement that rose within her, it was useless. She wanted him more than she'd ever wanted a man in her entire life.

Visibly put out by her husband's words, Eileen Johnson gave him a little push away from Lindee. "Just for that you're going to have to raise the ante tonight. I think another twenty-five thousand for her campaign coffers would be a good way of telling her that you're sorry you were so rude. Now before we leave you'll have to get out your checkbook and change the amount, you old cuss."

"Don't be ridiculous, Eileen. P.J. doesn't have to do that," Lindee protested. She felt like the wind had been knocked out of her sails. P.J.'s words had a ring of truth to them that had touched her. She took what he said as a gentle reminder to be careful. The next few days of this campaign she'd have to be on her guard.

"Oh, yes, he does, and he will," Eileen insisted, capturing Lindee's attention again. "Now come on, P.J., you've said quite enough for one night."

She watched them go and played over and over in her head what P.J. had said. Was that why she was so uneasy? If Brooks were helping Ted Bullock out there was no telling what could happen to her reputation, and even if she didn't want to believe Brooks would betray their relationship, Bullock surely had spies someplace nearby. She had to be careful. She just had to.

"Lindee, here's Mr. William Sutton. He's with Clayton Oil Company. Remember?" Earl smiled. "Oh, and Brooks has decided to film you after our guests go through the receiving line. No interview, just a picture of you and some of the guests. I'll tell you more later."

Mr. Sutton shook her hand, reminding her that he'd seen her last when she was a baby. After asking about her mother he began to tell a story about Lindee's father's campaigning, but Earl interrupted him.

"Lindee." A man in an expensively cut cowboy suit was grinning at her. He bent over and kissed her cheek. "I'm Billy Dean Harper. Jim sends his love and regrets that he couldn't be here. He had to fly to Washington for an unscheduled meeting, government business of some kind." He smelled like a rank combination of strong after-shave and day-old cigars as he resumed what Lindee imagined must be a perpetual grin.

Nowhere else but Texas, she thought when she looked down at the ring he wore on the middle finger of his right hand. It was a big diamond cut in the shape of Texas. Sparkling brightly, it stood out like a sore thumb, but it seemed to fit this man's personality. Cautioning herself to be gracious, Lindee was reminded that Jim Harper was one of the most influential men in Texas politics, having served in one capacity or another under three presidents after serving three terms as governor of the state. Billy Dean was his dear brother.

"Well, Mr. Harper, I'm certainly sorry Jim couldn't come, but I'm very pleased that you could make it." She smiled engagingly. She watched him take off in the direction of the champagne fountain.

Brooks talked quietly to his cameraman, making certain each move of the camera was precise and on target. Although he'd promised himself he wouldn't look at her, he couldn't keep his eyes from straying across the room. Earl was telling her about the film footage he wanted. Brooks had planned the next shots on the spur of the moment when he'd seen all the influential people fill the ballroom. Lindee's campaign needed a clever touch right now, and he thought he had a way to garner more attention for her. Perhaps the filming would get on national news. If he did it correctly, he knew it had a chance. And maybe afterward she'd talk to him.

Earl was busy arranging the scene as Brooks had asked. "Okay, Lindee, I need you to stand right over here. We're going to have P.J. come by, give you a nice big kiss on the cheek, shake your hand, and then he'll move out of the camera's way, and then Billy Dean will walk over and do the same thing. Meanwhile Brooks will be standing in front of you or beside you. I'm not quite sure about that part yet. He won't talk to you. He'll be talking to the camera, telling about the progress of your campaign."

"Okay," she agreed, suddenly as nervous as a beginner. Camera lights flickered on, and for a second Lindee blinked, reacting to the harsh glare. Then, after licking her lips, she smiled and waited for P.J. to come toward her.

"Here we go," Brooks's husky drawl boomed out across the room. "If the rest of you would be a little quieter I think we can capture some good quality sound here. And who knows, you might get to see yourselves on the news tomorrow."

103

Her own reaction startled her. Why she felt herself responding to the husky sound of his voice she had no idea, but nevertheless her heart trip-hammered a resoundingly strong beat. Maybe that was the way she had of reacting to the stress of the campaign. But she knew that wasn't the reason.

"Ready?" Brooks asked her, motioning to the cameraman as well as to P.J. "Be sure and watch the gentlemen who approach you. I wouldn't want your voters to know this scene was staged."

Forcing a smile, she reached for P.J.'s gnarled hand and held her composure as he grazed her cheek with his own. But Lindee hadn't missed Brooks's derisive tone of voice, and while she knew she shouldn't let it bother her, it did. Before she knew it P.J. had turned away and then Billy Dean Harper followed, the bright lights blazing behind him.

Then Brooks was standing with his back to her, his voice booming into the microphone. She couldn't get over the tingling sensation that ran through her whenever she saw him before the cameras like this. He was in total control in a very powerful way. Watching him perform for the lens was a little like watching a masterpiece being created.

With quick, slicing words he continued talking about her style of campaigning, and suddenly her ears burned with indignation. Not wanting to believe she was hearing him correctly, yet at the same time knowing she was right, it took all of her control not to slap the microphone out of his traitorous hand.

"Good evening," he said. "We're here at the Warwick Post Oak Hotel, Houston's answer to the famous Plaza, at a five-hundred-dollar-a-plate dinner honoring Lindee Bradley, Ted Bullock's thirty-year-old opponent. Miss Bradley has been steadily gaining attention in the polls and it looks as if she might stand a chance of unseating the incumbent. Now if her tactics seem a little strange—well, we've all heard of politicians kissing babies for votes." On the screen Lindee was kissing the men who streamed by her in what looked like a never ending procession. "Miss Bradley's tactics are unique, to say the least, and what she's doing does seem to be getting a great deal of attention."

Mockingly he turned back to her and smiled before closing. "And that's the way it's done here in Texas. I'm Brooks Griffin for WBCX."

Like a butterfly come to life she shook herself from the limbo she was in. The television lights were turned off. She heard Brooks thanking everyone, and still she tried to tell herself it hadn't happened.

Earl walked up to her, laughing and smiling. His expression changed when he looked down at her and saw her face.

"What in the hell is going on?" she spat. "Just exactly what is the meaning of that? Will you please tell me?"

"Oh, Lindee, don't be upset. Brooks decided to add that twist, hoping the national news might pick it up." He reached for her hand, but she quickly pulled it away. "Hey, wouldn't you like to see yourself on television all across the country?" His smile weakened. Earl could never stand to see her upset.

"What do you mean, national news, Earl?" her voice shook.

"He's working on a gimmick for voter identification for you. That's all." Seeing that she wasn't impressed, he kept talking nonstop, saying something about advertising and publicity and how good this exposure would be for all of them.

But Lindee didn't care about any of that right now. She was so angry she didn't trust herself to speak, too afraid her voice would falter and her eyes would fill with the tears that bubbled just below the surface. How could he? How could he have done this to her?

She hadn't seen Brooks come toward them, but she watched Earl's face fill with relief, and so she turned to see what had caused it. Smoothly Brooks began talking as if nothing out of the ordinary had happened. His voice had a warm, intimate sound to it.

"I think we got an excellent presentation there. It'll probably be good for a forty-five-second spot sometime tonight. My assistant's taking it to the station right now." He studied Lindee's face looking for some acknowledgment, but she looked like she might burst into tears. "I'm hoping the national news guys might see it and want to put it in for another touch of humor. It's worth a try, anyway."

"I want you out of my sight," she hissed. Her head was throbbing. "I want you off this campaign right now. I don't want you here. . . ." Temporarily she lost her frail train of thought when his eyes seared hers with a sudden explosive rage that was an equal match to her own. Stiffly she went on. "What you just staged was disrespectful—to me, to all women—and I resent it. I'm not in the habit of trading sex for votes, although it appears you'd like the voters of Texas to believe I am." Like a fast-moving tidal wave she kept talking, her words pouring out one on top of the other. "You have the nerve to brag about your clever publicity move. Who's it for? Me, or you?"

Suddenly he was through listening to her. Something was wrong between them, but for the life of him he didn't know what. "Why should this bother you?" he lashed out furiously. "I mean, it isn't as if you haven't been kissed by half the old men in the state by now, Lindee. Don't be a fool. That was never intended as anything except what it was. Disrespectful to women? I'm the last man in this room who'd want anything like that to happen. I'd think you knew me better!"

"That's enough." She glared at him. "I don't want you traveling with me on this campaign another minute. You've been against me from the very start, and I know it. I'll tell you one thing," she added vehemently, "you've overstepped your own ambition this time."

The room had grown quiet as more and more people had abruptly stopped their own conversations to try and catch a word or two of what was going on between Lindee and Brooks. But the two of them had held their fiery conversation in threatening undertones, and only the fuming anger in their faces gave any evidence of what was going on between them.

"You know what I think, Lindee. I think for some unknown reason . . ." He looked over at Earl, who was staring in amazement at the two of them. "I think you can't handle some things about yourself and you're looking for any excuse you can find to get rid of me." He eyed her intently. "If there was anything to your crazy accusations I might leave, but there's not and I'm not going anyplace." He could tell that it wouldn't do any good to argue with her anymore tonight. She was much too angry, but he hated what had erupted between them.

Lindee blinked, her eyes shot with a blaze of color and fire. Between clenched teeth she said, "Fun time is over, Brooks. Now get out of my way and out of my life. I don't want anything more to do with you."

She stalked away, through the blinding crush of people, ignoring the flashing light bulbs of the photographer's cameras, confused by his actions, knowing only that she might not be able to breathe ever again, the crushing weight inside her chest was so frightfully intense.

They missed the flight back to San Antonio and were forced to rent a private plane and hire a pilot. After leaving Brooks Lindee had been so distraught she couldn't think straight. Vehemently she'd demanded that he be dropped from the campaign. She'd shouted and ranted and stamped her foot every time Earl had tried to reason with her, giving all the reasons why it was a terrible mistake. And then for the first time in memory she'd made Earl angry with her, and she'd agreed to wait until the following morning to discuss it further.

After the flight they drove in uncomfortable silence through the treelined streets of San Antonio until they were in the King Williams area, a section of several long blocks of fine old homes belonging to some of the oldest members of San Antonio society. When they pulled into the circular driveway of Lindee's mother's Colonial house Lindee broke the silence. "I wonder why all the lights are on. It looks like she's having a party."

"Well, you know your mother," Earl said lightly, trying to distill the tension between them.

"Yes, well," she said. "Why don't you and Steve come in and have a nightcap? I promise not to say anything more about Brooks Griffin tonight." She tried to keep her voice smooth and

107

reassuring. She couldn't bear to hurt Earl's feelings. "Besides, Mother's counting on you two to stay in the guest house. She's so happy to have an excuse to open it up."

Earl reached over and took her hand in his. "Okay, Lindee. I'd like a nightcap."

The Bradley home was one of the loveliest around, having been carefully restored over the years in keeping with the period. If it was a little too commanding for Lindee, with its sixteen rooms, Olympic-size swimming pool, and two-story guest quarters, she didn't let it bother her for long. She didn't live in a home nearly this grand. Hers was a small, secluded country style house miles from here, private, quiet, and serene. She intended to keep it that way too. Vivian's party would come all too soon and the preparations would go on right up until the last minute. It seemed easier for Lindee to stay here now.

"Oh, darling, there you are. I was getting worried." Vivian hugged her at the door. "Earl, Steve, come right in here and fix yourselves a drink. I know you're all tired, but a little nightcap will do you good."

"What is all this, Mother?" Lindee heard voices and looked inside the huge living room to see several of the reporters who'd been following her campaign casually standing around.

"Well, I'll tell you, darling. It's just a gathering. Oh, I'm so happy you're home," she went on. She reached out and linked her arms into those of the two men. "Now, Earl, let's show Steve the bar. Lindee doesn't need any help."

"I thought I was going to have to go back to Houston and get you," Brooks sauntered up to her, a full drink in his hand. "What's the matter? Did you get lost?"

She ignored the look he gave her, conscious only of how her entire body was in shock at seeing him here in her own territory. Somehow she'd never even imagined she'd have to see him again, but that had been foolish thinking. "What are you doing here?"

"Ask Vivian. She'll tell you all about it. Meanwhile, what can I get you to drink?" He smiled that little-boy smile of his.

"Mother," she called, stalking over to where her mother stood talking to Earl. "What is going on here?"

"Oh, Lindee, you looked beautiful on the television tonight, dear." Vivian smiled exuberantly. "Well, I'll tell you. I drove to the airport and I gathered together all the people and invited them to stay in the guest house. Fun, huh?" She winked and went gaily off to join two of the San Antonio reporters.

Brooks walked up behind Lindee. She could smell the richness of his after-shave before she turned to look at him. "Can we talk?" he asked softly.

"How dare you? Even if my mother was crazy enough to invite you to stay here, the least you could have done was refuse."

"Brandy?" He handed her a snifter. "Vivian said you liked it."

"I asked you a question, and why do you insist upon calling her Vivian, like she's an old friend?" Lindee fairly shouted. She was seething inside, turmoil racing through her every nerve.

"Well, that's a lousy way to greet a man whom you've come to know so intimately." He shot her a mocking grin.

She wanted to slap him. "Answer my question."

"I dare because it so happens that Vivian and I *have* become friends." He took a sip from his drink and studied her response over the top of his glass. "I wasn't about to refuse when your mother so graciously invited me to stay here. Besides, I wanted to be close to the candidate." He smiled knowingly at her. "Don't tell me you don't understand that. Not after last night."

When she refused to answer him he went on. "I don't know what was going on in your head back there in Houston, but you're not going to get rid of me that easily. I'm not like any man you've known, Lindee. I won't be chased off."

Frustration washed over her, and anger and sorrow. She knew that if she stayed any longer she'd do something foolish then, like cry or let herself become snared by his charms once again. She wasn't up to any of this, not tonight.

"I hope you'll excuse me, Brooks. I have a terrible headache." Her words were cold and haughty. Abruptly she thrust her glass into his hand. "Good night."

She swung away while he watched her go, his mind consumed with the memory of her touch, her kiss, her caress. Then and there he vowed he'd wait her out. He didn't know what was wrong between them, but whatever it was they could work it out. They had to. What had begun as a conquest had become a full-blown obsession.

Being with her last night had only made things worse. He closed his eyes and flexed one hand open and shut, trying to calm the body that was betraying him. He wanted more than a few nights with Lindee, he now realized. He wanted much, much more.

CHAPTER SIX

Morning found her at her mother's breakfast table, impatiently tapping her foot. Earl and Steve were on the telephones, although they were supposed to have breakfast with her at eight o'clock sharp.

"More coffee, dear?" Vivian asked. "I'm sure they'll be here in just a minute and then we'll have our little talk. Oh, I've made all the arrangements for your boat trip down the San Antonio river tonight. They'll have Mexican food and an open bar. It's going to be lovely."

"I wish Earl and Steve would hurry. We're going to be off schedule today as it is." Actually, all Lindee wanted was to get the issue of Brooks out of the way. She'd had plenty of time to think about it. She felt like she'd been awake all night, and while she still felt that he wasn't good for her, she wasn't sure that Earl could be convinced. He'd frightened her last night when he'd become so angry. If she held firm and insisted upon Brooks leaving her campaign she was afraid she might jeopardize her friendship with Earl. It seemed to be a no-win proposition.

"Guess what?" Earl shouted as he charged into the room. "Listen to this." Before anyone could say a word he went on.

111

"CBS News is running Brooks's tape. It's on the midday report and it will appear on the evening report. How about that?"

"That's wonderful, just wonderful," Lindee said unenthusiastically.

He bent over and kissed the top of her head. "Oh, Lindee, can't you see? Brooks did just what he said he'd do. We're going to beat that Bullock yet. With this kind of publicity you're going to be totaling up votes faster than the Confederacy made dollar bills."

"That's the best news we've had in a long time." Vivian nodded. "It really is wonderful, Lindee."

"But I'm telling all of you that what Brooks did last night was intentionally demeaning. He didn't mean for it to turn out to be beneficial to me at all. He intended for me to be embarrassed." She looked at all three of their faces, but she could see that she wasn't getting through to them.

"Lindee, Earl told me about last night," her mother said quietly.

"Earl, Steve, I want to apologize for acting the way I did last night. I was angry, but I shouldn't have taken it out on you. I feel very badly about all of that."

"That's okay," Steve said.

"Well, what do you want to do, Lindee?" Sipping his coffee, Earl looked over the rim of his cup at her.

She could tell he wasn't giving up. "I'm willing to discuss it, but my feelings are still the same. I think Brooks Griffin should be kept as far away from my campaign as possible." The vehemence began to rise in her voice again, brought back to life by the memories of Brooks standing in front of the cameras last night.

"This is your campaign, Lindee. You run it like you see it," Earl answered softly. "I'll go along with you."

The hurt expression in his eyes made her want to cry. Damn Brooks. He'd caused all of this.

"Lindee, you made all the Texas television stations as well as the national ones. What more could you ask for, dear? Even if you aren't crazy about him, your public recognition is rising as fast as can be," Vivian reasoned.

"I want him out of this campaign more than I've ever wanted anything in a long time."

"Well then, you do what you think is best," Earl spoke up. "But I've got one more thing to say. Whatever you think Brooks did to you last night, he didn't make you look bad. Maybe he made you look a little funny, but he knew what he was doing and it worked."

They sat looking glumly at one another for a long time. As much as she hated it, she had to give in. She'd rather do almost anything than lose Earl's friendship, and the way it looked she was going to lose it if she insisted upon Brooks's exclusion.

"All right, he stays." She watched them smile. "He's going to get one more chance." She knew as sure as she was sitting there that she'd live to regret it, but she looked over at Earl and knew she was powerless to choose any other option.

"I'll tell him what you said," Earl offered.

"You won't need to say anything to him, Earl. It's quite evident that he didn't take me very seriously anyway. I saw him here last night." The look in Earl's eyes told her to go easy. It would be better for them all if she kept quiet about Brooks from now on. She'd agreed to let him stay and now she must promise to keep her complaints to herself. It would be nearly an impossibility, she thought.

Throughout the day Lindee found herself constantly searching people's faces looking for Brooks. She hadn't seen him since she'd stormed away from him the night before, and by the time her scheduled dinner party on the San Antonio river began she found herself wondering if perhaps he'd followed her request and had taken off for Houston.

"Wishful thinking," she said aloud when the party started. He stood at the boat's gangplank with his back to her, greeting her guests as if he were the host.

All the arrangements had been made well ahead of time and

everything was going like clockwork. The party had been her idea. A boat ride through the heart of San Antonio with a mariachi band, good food and good drinks for all the reporters, cameramen, and photographers who'd followed her campaign. This was one way Lindee knew of thanking all those who'd traveled with her, getting up many days before dawn and finishing late in the evenings. It was their job, but they'd been kind to her throughout the trip and she wanted to repay that kindness.

The evening was beautiful. A light breeze blew down the meandering river, stirring the abundance of fall flowers and bounty of trees on its banks in gentle movement. The guests were gathered at the Palacio Hilton, where men in white coats greeted each female guest with a colorful fresh flower, and as each guest boarded the boat chilled margaritas lined with salt and lime were thrust into their waiting hands.

The women wore festive dresses with a decided Mexican touch. Mr. George, a well-known local dress designer, had selected a lovely dress for Lindee from his shop. Called a San Antonino, it had been made in the village of San Antonino outside Oaxaca, Mexico. The ankle-length yellow dress was short-sleeved with intricate colored embroidery on the yoke, around the armhole, and down the front. A row of stick figures under the yoke were what separated its design from all the others. It was believed that the stick figures represented romantic messages being sent by its designer. A myth, but a delightful one. Lindee loved the dress. On her wrist she wore an extremely wide gold bracelet, and she had long circular earrings that matched. She wore a yellow flower in her hair, tucked in just above her ear. The casual attire went hand in hand with the casual evening.

She could tell by the noise level that it was going to be fun. Reporters were known for enjoying free drinks and good food, and Lindee had arranged to have an abundance of both. Mariachis played beautiful love ballads on the far side of the boat, while in the center two long tables were set up with food and drinks. The boat was to travel down the river for two hours before returning to the hotel.

114

Greeting her guests gave her the opportunity to make certain that she and Brooks were never around each other for any length of time. He looked magnificent in a wheat-colored linen jacket over a light-blue silk shirt, and wheat-colored slacks. Going along with the relaxed mood of the party, he had the sleeves of his jacket pushed up along his lower arm, a style she'd seen on other men and thought nothing about. On him it looked offhandedly spectacular. Always, she thought, always he managed to look strong and in control. No matter where he was, no matter what he was doing, he never seemed to be off balance. He looked like a man who had all the answers.

The night moved forward and Lindee was having as good a time as anyone. One of the local television reporters who'd been invited to join them had come, camera and all. Lindee had watched the reporter work her way around the boat asking innocuous questions of the guests. When the camera swung toward her Lindee knew that now it was her time. With a smile she greeted the reporter.

"Good evening and welcome. We're glad you could join us."

"Thank you. It's good to be here." The reporter smiled profusely, giving the camera all the benefit of her look. "I was wondering if you'd answer a question or two, Miss Bradley, for our local viewers."

The way she said it made it sound a little patronizing, but Lindee merely smiled her agreement. This woman was fast developing a reputation as a barracuda, and Lindee felt it best just to answer her questions and be done with it.

"Certainly."

"I understand you've come back to San Antonio for a big party your mother's giving tomorrow night. Is that right?"

"Yes and no," Lindee said, looking into the camera's eye. "I've come back to campaign as well as to attend my mother's party."

"Are we invited? I'm sure the viewers would like to see what a big gala your mother has planned."

"Of course." Lindee nodded, mentally giving credit to the reporter. She had got what she wanted.

"One more question, Miss Bradley. Is there any truth to the rumor that you and Mr. Griffin, the newsman from WBCX in Houston, are fast becoming more than friends?"

If the question had come from anyone else she might not have been so disturbed, but the way the woman let her voice linger over her last few words left no doubt what was actually in her mind. Lindee shifted her eyes toward Brooks and then back full face to the camera. "Absolutely no truth. None whatsoever. Thank you, Miss Barrera." She stood her ground.

Not two minutes after the reporter left Lindee heard Brooks's voice as he came softly up behind her. "You know, I love this town of yours. Once when I was just getting started I was assigned to come here to do a report on the Fiesta River Parade. As I recall it was one big three-day party." He walked over to the edge of the slow-moving boat, turned, and leaned his back against the railing, looking only at her, ignoring the view of the beautifully lighted sites along the river bank.

Straightening her shoulders, Lindee didn't move, although he was leaning too close to her, his arms maintaining his balance against the railing, his hips swaying forward in an intriguing stance. If he said anything about the two of them and their relationship, she swore before the heavens that she was going to give him a piece of her mind and be done with it, here and now. That female reporter's question had only served to seal Lindee's resolve. Brooks had to stay out of her life.

"Are you going to talk to me or not? Earl told me all about your meeting." He stared into her eyes, trying to figure out where it was going, this mixed-up relationship that had developed between them. "Lindee, I swear to God I didn't intend to embarrass you last night."

"How could you have done that, Brooks? How could you?" she replied shakily.

"Dammit all, woman, you're the only one who thinks that what I did was wrong. Don't tell me you don't know that you made national news. I hear you may get a national interview. I did that just to help. . . ." He stopped himself. His words reverberated in his ears, sounding too close to pleading. "But I'll be damned if I'll beg you to believe me," he said in the coldest of voices.

"I'm trying to get along with you, Brooks, so let's just forget it, shall we?"

"How can we forget it? Huh? You don't believe me. You don't believe Earl or your mother. Just who do you trust, Lindee?" he replied gruffly, his voice scraping across her nerves like sandpaper. "You don't even seem able to trust yourself!"

"Okay, okay," she said, taken back by the force of his sudden volatile words. "Let's just drop it. I am trying very hard to trust Earl and my mother's beliefs."

Nothing more was said between them. Instead, they both took in the sights and sounds of the evening.

Finally she spoke, vowing to herself that for Earl's sake she'd have to go along with Brooks, tolerate him, give him the benefit of the doubt. And she had to think it strange how vehemently he'd protested his innocence. "What did you like best about San Antonio? The river, the music, food, what?"

"The women. I liked the women best." He began laughing. "San Antonio has beautiful women." He looked at her then, still smiling. He watched her eyes, trying to decipher all that he could read there, but they only looked sad, and he didn't think that could be possible. Surely she'd felt it, too, that magic that they'd shared that night. For two days he'd thought about it, mulled it over in his mind, studied it, analyzed and reflected. It was special. There was no denying it. Now he wanted to be with her, only her, but obviously she wasn't thinking the same thing.

"That's very interesting. Maybe you can do one of your commentaries on the beautiful women you've met." Her words came out caustic, causing a smile to play across his lips. "Excuse me, won't you. I need to attend to my other guests. I hope you're having a good time, Brooks."

He caught her arm as she began to move away. "Not so fast.

You've been avoiding me, Lindee, but that's okay. I'm more or less getting used to that." He loosened his grip, running his thumb along her inner arm, bringing back memories that floated between both of them like seductive music. For the briefest instant they were all alone, off in some distant place. "I want to be with you tonight. You tell me how."

She shook her head, first mildly and then with a violent shake. "No."

"What do you mean?" He looked all around, but they were alone. Nobody was near them. He felt a twinge of anger spark to life. "Do you mean no to tonight or what?"

"No, never." She looked at him then, sure of what she had to say, wishing with all her heart she didn't have to. "For us it ended the night we shared, Brooks. That was an insane thing for me to have done."

In shock he let go of her and turned so that his back was to her, his dark eyes staring straight ahead out into the still water.

"Look, Brooks, despite what happened last night I haven't forgotten about that night. Please don't think I blame you entirely for what happened between us. It was a case of dual participation." A weak smile flashed across her face and disappeared as quickly as it came. "But it was a very destructive thing for me to have involved myself in. While I may be guilty of succumbing to my own physical desires, I'm not in the habit of placing myself in jeopardy like I did with you, and Brooks, please believe me, I won't do it again. Even if you're not against me, we have no future. This election is all that matters to me right now."

He gripped the railing until his knuckles were white, and when he spoke his words were as sharp as a saber. "My God, woman, you make it all sound like some high-level court case instead of what it really was." He shot her a look of bitter rage as he turned to face her, then cut his eyes away from her. "Dual participation —that's a good one. I'll try to remember that." His voice softened then. "What we shared was special—or at least I thought so." He shook his head in disbelief. "Dual participation," he said with a dry laugh. "You really have a way with words."

"Please, Brooks. You and I both can agree that we got caught up in the moment, the mood of the evening. I told you before I didn't want anything to happen between us. Okay, it did." She nodded. "And I'm accepting my share of the responsibility. But I'm saying that it won't happen again. I don't trust you, Brooks. You're ambitious, enormously so, and I don't have any idea where that ambition may lead. For two days I've found my heart in my throat worrying about whether you'd reveal our night together to one of your cronies and have it end up being front-page news. I don't intend to be used by you, Brooks. I can't take that chance right now."

A deep despairing sense of futility gripped him. Was this the same woman he'd held in his arms so brief a time ago? It couldn't be.

"You've got to stay away from me. We shouldn't even be seen together talking like this now. Just a few minutes ago, I had to dodge questions about you and me. Are you actually hoping you'll sabotage my chances of winning this election?" She looked straight at him and then down to where he gripped the railing. "I haven't decided the answer to that question yet."

He studied her face, his eyes looking for a reaction, a hint of regret, a brief straying of a glance that would tell him she didn't mean what she was saying. "Do you mean you can stand there and tell me it meant nothing to you—our being together the other night? Can you honestly say that?"

She said nothing.

"Well, hell, it looks like I really misjudged it all, Lindee, but for me it was the most . . ." He couldn't find the words to tell her that he'd never wanted a woman with such a burning intensity before, and he'd never had a woman treat him like she was. It was almost too much for him to believe.

She'd turned her head away, unwilling to face him. Living with this newfound pain was one thing, but keeping herself under control was another.

"Look at me," he demanded, his voice shaking with rage.

Steadfastly she kept her eyes averted. Facing him right now

119

would be her downfall. Tears stung her eyes, and it took all her might not to let them fall.

After a few uncomfortable moments he spoke, his voice menacingly low and as icy as a winter's snowstorm blowing hard against her face. "It was a game to you, wasn't it? One of your whims, a mood. Have fun with the guy tonight. You can always find an excuse to force him into keeping his distance tomorrow."

"No," she replied, hating herself for answering him but hurt at his implication.

"Lindee, the local reporters want one more picture before we call it a night. When do you want to do it?" Earl had come up behind them. The boat had docked.

"Right now, Earl. We're all through here," she said and she began following him to the center of the boat, trying to conceal her shaking body.

"Maybe you're through, but I'm not," Brooks hissed.

She turned in time to see him stalk off the boat, everything about him radiating hostility, from the hard sharp line of his jaw to the abrupt edge in his walk.

Brooks had the look of a wild man when he left, but she was in even worse shape. She had to face all the guests, saying her good-byes, accepting good-spirited thanks. Somehow she pulled herself together, calmed her shaking hands, performing her role as the gracious hostess and candidate. She even managed an excited look for the photographers who'd lined up for one last shot of her leaving the boat.

But all she wanted to do was get home, away from everyone. She was on the verge of tears when she got out of the car and bid Earl and Steve good night. She walked slowly toward the darkened house through the back way, along the brick sidewalk her father had laid with loving hands when she was just a young girl.

"Lindee." Brooks's voice shot out in the quiet darkness and she jumped with fright.

She saw him then, standing in the shadows next to a rose

trellis, his familiar form outlined by the light of the moon. He stepped out onto the brick walk.

"I want to talk to you."

"We've said it all, Brooks. There's no need in prolonging this another minute." Appalled by what she suddenly felt, Lindee only knew she didn't want to talk to him. Already tonight he'd managed to awaken a new level of awareness in her—a terrible combination of desire and fear that she wanted to be rid of. It was all too painful.

Now she knew she held the power to let her life become hopelessly entangled with his. He'd as much as said so earlier. With one wrong word, one mistaken movement, she could acquiesce and take the chance of bringing down destruction on both of them and their careers, careers they'd struggled so hard to establish.

"Lindee, you can't mean what you said before. I don't believe you could mean that." He wasn't finished with her. He couldn't let her dismiss him as she'd done, accusing him of being something that he wasn't, wordlessly telling him that their night together had meant nothing to her.

His voice carried in it such vulnerability that she longed to reach out for him. Then and there she knew the naked truth. She cared for him, really cared. She wanted much more than one night with this startling man. And as her feelings were realized Lindee knew with an even greater conviction that she must protect them both. If Brooks couldn't see how his career might be damaged she'd have to help him see it, somehow. She didn't want him to be hurt either.

He grabbed her. "Tell me, damn it."

He was shaking her then, and she didn't have to look into his eyes to see how angry he was. She could feel it as his fingers held her so tightly she wanted to cry out. But she waited.

Then he let go of her arms and brought his hands up to her face. Tenderly he held her there, his hands cupping her chin. His lips came down to claim hers in the gentlest of ways. And maybe if his kiss had been rough or demanding she could have fought

121

him off, but he was nothing but tender and loving. Every part of her was set afire like a dry forest by a match. Oh, how she longed to reach out to him.

His tongue sought hers, and despite herself she didn't resist as they met and dueled. She closed her eyes and desire washed over her like an unrelenting storm. She felt her knees weaken in reaction to the feel of his body pressing softly against hers. When he wrapped his arms around her, letting his lips continue to arouse her, she knew that just as she'd discovered how much she cared about him, all she really wanted now was to respond to the passion of the moment, to find once again that magical intimacy that they had shared before. Her body was going crazy with its own responses.

As his hands began a delicate exploration of her body, his mouth increased its pressure, deeply drawing her in nearer and nearer to the point where passion overrides reason. She felt a tremor of longing ripple through her as he pressed the hard line of his body closer to the softness of her own. She couldn't breathe. Her head was pounding with the desire that had sparked and then intensified as his hands roamed over the swell of her breasts and the warmth of her legs. She wanted more.

Suddenly she was dizzy, her thoughts spinning away from the hunger of her body. "Stop it," she reacted, pulling abruptly away from him. Something in her had snapped, and from some part of her she didn't even know about, a surge of strength bolted through her. "We can't do this." Tears stung her eyes. "I can't do this."

Surprised, almost dazed, Brooks looked down at his hand. He'd ripped her dress when she'd jerked away. How, he didn't know, but it was torn from the shoulder down. "Lindee," he said, and looked at her dress, confusion clouding his eyes.

"No, no, no," she cried, shaking uncontrollably. "It's not going to happen. Understand me?" She glanced at her dress and then back at him. They were both bordering on becoming dangerously out of control. Emotions stood between them like a dancing wall of flame. She didn't give the dress another thought, nor whether they might be heard or seen. She had to lash out at him, drive him away while she still had the strength. It was now or never.

"I want you to stay away from me. You have to." Reluctant tears dropped down from her eyes, first one and then another, until they were cascading down her face. She ached with the pain in her heart. "It's all too complicated."

"No, it's not. You're trying your damnedest to make it complicated. Look, I want to be with you. What is it going to hurt?" he implored. "What in the hell can it hurt?"

"Everything and everyone."

"That's . . . that's just so much bull. If you don't want to be with me, why can't you just come out and say so? Is it really because you don't trust me?"

"I've told you before what I thought about you!"

"Well, that's not good enough." He scowled. "You've been wrong from the beginning." Brooks Griffin had been in Vietnam, he'd fought many a battle in his career to get where he was, but he just couldn't talk to the woman who stood before him. His insides were going haywire and the words he wanted to say remained inside his head, piling up one on top of the other like so many useless bricks.

She made her voice hard and firm. "Brooks, listen to me. Even if I did trust you, and I didn't think you wanted to see me lose this election, let's look at it from a purely professional slant. I've tried to explain this from my point of view—now maybe you'll be able to see it from your own. You know you could be ruined by your own reporter's code—a conflict of interest. Isn't that what they call it in journalism?"

He listened, every now and then shaking his head. It was no use. He was powerless.

She felt like a deranged woman now, saying unreasonable things, only certain that she desperately wanted to make him understand.

"Oh, I can see it all now. Once we start sleeping together," she charged blindly on, "you'd agree to start making me look good.

123

Keep me happy. Give me good press. Oh, yes, I can see it. What was it you said to me before? I don't know . . . something about helping each other and having fun together," she sputtered. "Anyway, what you meant was that we could trade favors. That's what you wanted. You even let me know how we could keep everything a secret between us. Well, it won't work, Brooks. You could be ruined as quickly as I could." She was sobbing now. "You could lose your reputation as a professional just as I could lose the election, and then we'd both be left with nothing but hate for one another. Is that what you want?"

None of what she was saying about his using her was true, but he couldn't convince her of it. The only lucid thing she'd said was about their careers. And maybe it was the pain in her voice, he thought, but something had made him listen to her, and she was right. For the first time he could see it. He ran his fingers through his hair, a longtime habit. It wasn't only possible but highly probable that he could be used against her in this damned campaign of hers. He was tearing her apart. He could see it now. The agony in her eyes and her face told him more than he wanted to know.

Well. He sighed. He could handle it. If she didn't need him, if their night together had meant so little to her, and if there was any possibility that he might damage her chances to win this election and his own professional credibility, it would be best for both of them if he left her alone.

There was nothing more to be said. With one last look at her face he turned and walked slowly away. He could still hear her sobbing, but he didn't let himself turn back. A twinge of sadness gripped him, making silence his only ally. And as her cries faded away with each step he took a shocking sense of shame invaded him. One by one, in fast-forward motion, he remembered all the times he'd virtually forced her into being with him. He remembered their first kiss on the balcony of her hotel room, the night when he'd barged in on her in the hot tub and followed her persistently to her room. Remorse stalked him as he thought of what agony he could have caused this undeserving woman.

And the most damning thing about it was that he knew he might never have listened to her still if she hadn't forced him to think about his own career and how it could be damaged. Only her sobbing, desperate appeal regarding his own future had brought reality down upon his head. No wonder she hated him.

Lindee couldn't believe her eyes. He was walking away from her without another word. Suddenly, as sad as she felt, a red-hot fury overcame her. It was all too maddening, the way he was acting. Once she'd told him about how their being together might ruin his own precious career, he'd sauntered away without another word. Her darkest fears nudged at her, reminding her of his ambitious ways. Well, Brooks Griffin would just have to find another headliner. She was through. It was finished.

By the next day her feelings still hadn't calmed. All night long she'd tossed and turned, not quite able to lull herself to sleep, in spite of her need. Every time she thought about Brooks she became furious all over again. He was incorrigible, but that didn't seem quite as important as the knowledge that she cared for him.

But there were too many things to be done to let him monopolize her every thought. Last-minute details for the party kept Vivian busy while Lindee spent the time going over her campaign plans with Earl and Steve. Even though the sky was overcast the weatherman had promised no rain for San Antonio, although terrible storms had hit other parts of the state. Vivian had called the local weather channel repeatedly, swearing she'd die if a drop of rain fell on her party.

In the middle of the afternoon Lindee walked past the library window on her way upstairs. Hearing noises, she looked out to see Brooks and several other reporters along with a few of her staff playing touch football on the lawn. She stood there staring out for a minute, lost in her own mental hazings. She couldn't help but notice the way Brooks had of gaining the friendship of everyone around him as well as their respect. She watched as Steve ran up and patted Brooks on the shoulder and she thought of how her staff adored him. How could it be that everyone else pictured him as an honorable man while she alone knew him for what he really was? Why was she the only one? It didn't quite make sense.

Brooks sat down in the grass alongside Earl, grabbing the chance for a free afternoon before the party. He hadn't seen Lindee all day except from a distance. He couldn't predict how she'd react or even how he would when next they met. All he knew was that he surprised himself.

Thinking he could take it all in stride had been a mistake, but then it seemed he'd been making lots of mistakes since he'd met Lindee. He was upset, surprisingly so. Banishing her from his thoughts was impossible. Lindee had touched a chord deep inside him and then gripped him with an amazing strength. She had really awakened his emotions and he wasn't willing to put them to rest without her. He was in love.

The party that night was like something out of an old Hollywood movie. Gallons of champagne, enough uniformed maids and butlers to assure that no one stood for a minute without a drink, exotic food in abundance, and fresh flowers everywhere.

"You look smashing, dear," Lindee's mother told her when she came down the curved staircase into the huge entry hall. And with the fine champagne they toasted the evening. "Smile and enjoy yourself, Lindee. I want this to be your very special night," her mother said before giving her a kiss on the cheek.

And silently Lindee vowed she'd try.

"Oh, one thing more, dear. There's someone special coming tonight. I can't wait for you to meet her. I'm so honored that she's agreed to come. It's Katrina McAllister."

"Really?" Lindee couldn't have hidden her surprise even if she'd wanted to.

"Yes, she phoned me this morning. You know she's one of the richest oilwomen in Texas, maybe the world. She's smart, frightfully clever, and everyone agrees she's one of the most attractive

126

women in the state. That's why she's in all the Texas magazines so often."

"Well, I can't wait to meet her, Mother. I've always hoped to one day."

"Your chance will come soon enough. I'm anxious to see what you think of her. Watch for her. She has that dark, dark hair and those high cheekbones. Oh, I think you'll know her when you see her. Anyway, I don't believe half the stories I've heard about her," Lindee's mother went on. "If they were all true she'd have to have lived a hundred years already and she's only a few years older than you, dear."

"I'm looking forward to this," Lindee exclaimed before reaching for a glass of bubbling champagne.

Once the band began to play in the dining room, which had been emptied for dancing, Lindee stood in the receiving line greeting her mother's guests. Dressed in a luxurious gown of sweater-woven white cotton designed by Valentino, she looked the perfect part of the sophisticated lady, as the press had named her. Long-sleeved, narrowing down to her ankles, the gown reminded Lindee of fire and ice. All along the bodice and sleeves lavish fiery beading had been sewn so that wherever she turned, whatever she did, lights sparkled all around her. Diamond earrings and a matching bracelet composed of a strand of small diamonds finished off her gown, and she'd curled her long thick hair and piled it atop her head beguilingly. She was a photographer's dream, so much so that the light from popping flashbulbs interfered with her vision.

"Here's Katrina asking for you," her mother said, smiling at the beautiful Katrina Longoria McAllister, who was standing there.

"Hello, Lindee. It's good to meet you." Katrina smiled.

"I'm so sorry I've never had the opportunity to meet you before. I feel I've missed something." Lindee sighed. "I've wanted to meet you for such a long time."

"You're very kind," Katrina said in a deep, throaty voice that Lindee thought must be the sexiest she'd ever heard. "Well, I know how busy you must be, but why don't you and I share a drink together right now? Would that be agreeable with you?" The woman smiled a dazzling smile that lit up her face. Dressed in a delicate gown of gold-colored silk crepe, Katrina was breathtaking. A couture dress that was clasped on one shoulder with a large oval diamond set with rubies, the gown was designed so that it left the other shoulder bare, accentuating her pale olive complexion.

Lindee admired this woman who didn't look a bit older than herself. She seemed tough and warm all at the same time. Intriguing was the only word that came to mind. And when Lindee watched her talking to another guest and laughing that deep, throaty laugh of hers, all she could do was stare in fascination. Every woman in the world must envy her, Lindee thought, watching how she commanded the attention of the people standing around them.

"A toast," Katrina said, and laughingly reached out and took two filled champagne glasses from a passing maid.

Lindee took the glass from her and waited. It was Katrina McAllister's show right now, and Lindee was content just to watch her.

"To Lindee Bradley, future state senator. May she be a faithful representative," she said, and tapped Lindee's glass with her own.

"And I'd like to propose a toast to the most exciting lady here tonight." Brooks stood watching them both. He looked stunning in his white coat and tails, very much the celebrity that he was on the verge of becoming.

Lindee let her eyes meet his for the briefest moment and automatically raised her glass, feeling her cheeks redden. It was the first time she'd been near him since last night, and a rush of emotions assaulted her.

"To Katrina McAllister, who knows how to live life to the fullest," he said.

Katrina seemed as surprised as Lindee. They both assumed

he'd toast Lindee, and Lindee's expression showed it. But Katrina never seemed to give Lindee another thought.

"Prove it, Mr. Griffin, by dancing with me." Katrina took his glass from his hand and set both of them down at a nearby table. "We'll speak again, Lindee," she said, never taking her eyes away from Brooks as he pulled her to him and walked with her in the direction of the band.

Lindee stood perfectly still, rooted to the spot. How humiliating, she thought, and then forced a smile to her face. She wasn't about to let Brooks think it had bothered her in the least. He'd chosen his headliner for the night now that Lindee had let him know she wasn't going to cooperate.

Earl walked up then. "Dance with me?"

"I'd love it." He held her hand and escorted her into the middle of the room. Lindee didn't bother to look around. She closed her eyes and let her feet follow his moves.

And for the rest of the night she tried to convince herself that she didn't care that Brooks seemed to enjoy the attentions Katrina was bestowing upon him. She even tried to smile whenever she caught him looking her way, as if nothing he did could bother her. But she couldn't deny it to herself as time and time again the hurt and the humiliation attacked her, and every time she heard Brooks's deep laugh or Katrina's sexy one, she only knew she wanted the night to end.

CHAPTER SEVEN

When the rain begain pouring down the next day Vivian Bradley said it was a good sign—a sign that the weather had been cooperating with her to make her party an even bigger success than she'd imagined. Lindee's memories of the night weren't quite as warm as her mother's, but she remained quiet. The fact that she'd been miserable throughout the entire evening had nothing to do with Vivian.

Something had happened last night when she'd seen Brooks and Katrina together. An all-consuming piercing shot of jealousy had struck her as hard as any bullet. It was a new experience, one she despised. Nothing would have pleased her more than to have separated the two of them in the severest of ways. Lindee had hated them both.

However, politics was the focal point of her attentions, and the rainy day found her inside the library with Earl and Steve, trying to ignore the sounds around the house of people cleaning up from the gala affair.

"Bullock's wavering, thinking about changing his mind. He told one of his aides he doesn't want to go on with the debate scheduled between you two, Lindee. It's all very private, hush-hush. He doesn't want it leaked to the press yet. Says it wouldn't do him any good with the voters to debate you." Earl adjusted his glasses.

She looked at him. "He's chicken."

"That's what I said. We're supposed to get his final answer later today," Earl said.

"He might be making a big mistake by not debating me. Don't you think?" she asked, already knowing the answer.

"Yep. That's probably part of the reason why he doesn't want anything told to the press. I look for him to change his mind after he's had time to think it over and talk to his people."

"You know, Lindee, you don't even have to do this debate if you don't want to," Steve spoke up. "I think you've got him going good right now. That's why he's afraid to debate you, afraid of sticking his neck out at this time."

"Well, let's just let him squirm for a while. When he contacts us to agree to the debate tell him we reserve the right to choose the time and date. I want to do it this week. Otherwise he'll spend all his predebate time gathering publicity for himself with more of his wild accusations. Let's not give him any time to do that. When we decide when we'll do it, we'll call the television stations first and then notify him."

Steve shook his head. "You're amazing. Did you know that?"

Earl agreed, laughing. "Some of these old-timers who consider themselves professional politicians should study your strategy."

She didn't reply. It was true about her progress. Playing the game was becoming more and more easy for her and now there were many indicators saying the challenger had a fifty-fifty chance of defeating the incumbent.

Bullock called that night, and as promised, Lindee had the TV stations notified and then informed Bullock she would debate him in three days.

By the time she finished the debate, she was certain that she was a strong contender, feeling the first waves of political elation course through her as she accepted congratulations all around. The TV studio lights were bright, creating a stifling heat that only added to the tension that had built up around the two candidates. But she'd handled Bullock brilliantly, or at least that's what Earl had termed it. She'd taken issue after issue, exposing his shallow way of thinking for all the viewers to see. Forcing him to admit that his support of his own women's rights bill had been reluctant at best, she'd ended the debate with an appeal to all the voters to cast their ballots based on their convictions that it was time for good government to rule in the state of Texas.

The only incident that marred the evening was with Brooks. He'd ignored her since the night of the dinner on the river when they'd extinguished the possibility of anything more happening between them. When he'd flirted with Katrina at Vivian's party, it had hurt her badly—Lindee thought she could bear the silence of their relationship much easier than she could stand seeing him with another woman. The incident had only served to reinforce her feelings of isolation.

But a new dimension had been added when she'd seen Brooks with Ted Bullock before the scheduled debate, the politician's arm thrown casually around Brooks's shoulder as they stood posing for a picture together. And when she'd overheard Bullock raving on camera about Brooks being the finest newscaster in the state, she was seething. What stronger reminder did she need than to see the two of them laughing and talking together like an uncle and his favorite nephew? Brooks wanted Bullock to win the election. He had all along, and while she told herself it wasn't news, she felt a fresh layer of sadness gently cover her heart.

Determined to hold herself together, exhausted by the long hours of the campaign itself, and torn up inside from the depression that engulfed her, Lindee felt she had no choice. She told herself the same things over and over again when she crawled between the cool, fresh sheets of her bed much later that night. The only possible thing to do was to stop herself from thinking. She must shut down her mind, refuse each random thought that tried to gain entry, and block away all memory of the past. In effect, she must become an automaton, performing as necessary but only on the most superficial of levels, except where the voters were concerned. She had to, in order to survive the ordeal right now.

And she did. Too busy to notice, Earl and the others on her staff carried forth through the next day. Only Vivian Bradley saw beyond the facade and said so.

Lindee and her mother were having their lunch. It was three o'clock in the afternoon, but another hectic morning had made them postpone all thoughts of food. "And how's it going for you, my dear?" Vivian asked, showing concern.

"Never better." Lindee smiled lightly. "Earl says we're rolling now. My interview with CBS has been pushed up to five thirty today, and the opinion polls say I'm on the verge of overtaking Bullock. I've got one last commercial to do and that's about it."

"Wonderful," her mother said. And then, putting down her forkful of chicken salad, she asked, "And Brooks Griffin. How's it going between you two?" It seemed perfectly natural for her to ask—after the fiasco back in Houston when Lindee had tried to get rid of him.

"That's an issue I don't even want to discuss, Mother." She was careful to keep the anger from her voice. Indifference was more in order. At least that's what she hoped her mother would hear.

"I see. Although I'll admit I'm a little surprised. The better I get to know him the more I think you complement each other perfectly." Vivian studied her daughter's face for a long while. "There's something bothering you, Lindee. You're not yourself lately."

"I'm exhausted, that's all," Lindee argued. "I'm so tired." Burning tears lodged in her eyes, and she was stung by a return of all her jumbled feelings. "I'm trying my best, believe me."

"You mean with the campaign?"

Lindee nodded.

"Listen, darling, you sound as if you're apologizing in case you don't win." Vivian's tone became pleading. "Oh, Lindee," she went on, searching for understanding. "You seem to have forgotten. This is your dream, not mine, not Earl's, but yours, and nobody is going to take over your dream. Just remember, we—Earl and I, the people around you—got on your bandwagon because we believed in you."

Lindee stared uncomprehendingly.

Calmly her mother continued. "I don't really care two hoots about your being senator right now—no matter what I've said. I know how hard it all is. I went through it with your father, remember?"

Nodding, Lindee let her eyes meet those of her loving mother. She longed to go and put her head down on her lap and tell her of all her conflicting feelings. But she merely smiled.

"You're going to be somebody special one day soon, Lindee. To me you already are. But when it happens it's going to change all our lives, and I can wait, believe me. Whatever happens will happen soon enough. Don't ever forget you were the one who started this race, and we all went along with you, not because of the race itself but because of you." A deep sigh sounded through the room. "I'm going to always love you, no matter what happens. And in the end love is all that matters. It's the beginning and the end. Everyone needs to be loved, Lindee."

She stood up and Lindee could only marvel at the wisdom in her mother's words. It was as if a huge weight had been lifted from Lindee's shoulders. It made no difference what she did. She was loved for herself.

Vivian went over and hugged her. "I've got to have my beauty rest, darling. Earl said the reporter from CBS might want to interview me, and I can't have him thinking I look old enough to be your grandmother, now, can I?"

Lindee let herself respond to her mother's embrace. It was good, this new feeling of hers. It had been a long time, it seemed, since she'd felt anything, anything at all.

"Get some rest yourself, dear. A thirty-minute nap would do wonders for you."

The interviewer from CBS was Elizabeth Royal, a bright

134

young woman Lindee had met once before. The living room had been arranged for the program, furniture had been moved out, the lights had been set up, and Lindee had even agreed to a little pancake makeup applied to her face. Miss Royal had laughingly assured Lindee she might look sick without it.

At first it all went well. Elizabeth Royal had come prepared, and the questions she asked were direct ones Lindee considered to be quite fair. It was only at the end of the interview, when the woman reported the latest polls predicting a major upset in Lindee's favor, that she felt the dismal sweep of sadness overwhelm her once again. She could hardly pay attention to the woman's words for the unhappiness that had taken over her senses. She fought back, trying her best to find the enthusiasm that should be there right now. Everything was going her way. Perhaps destined to be the next freshman state senator. That was the way the interviewer closed out the segment. But somehow the thrill wasn't there. It had disappeared somewhere along the way.

Brooks was there. He waited until she'd finished the segment with the woman from CBS before approaching her.

"Lindee, you know I promised my viewers another interview. Do you think you could give me a five-minute conversation right now?" He kept his voice in a low monotone, hoping he'd sound professionally indifferent as he dealt with her. "You're already set up, really. Just stay where you are and I'll get Mike over here. What do you say?"

Her entire body began to shake involuntarily, and she nodded her agreement, folding her arms in front of her chest so that he couldn't see her quivering hands. It was the first time he'd spoken to her, the first she'd seen of him, since Katrina McAllister had so effectively captivated him.

He left, and she listened to the noisy confusion as the people from CBS moved into another part of the house to interview Vivian. Lindee tried not to think about Brooks, hoping she could calm herself down, and so she tried to think about her mother instead. But it did no good at all.

Unable to concentrate, still reeling with the wealth of emotions Brooks had reintroduced merely by talking to her, Lindee sat dejectedly waiting. Why was it that he maintained that kind of influence over her? She wouldn't have believed it before, but now the electricity that pulsed through her was enough to assure her that it was true. She wasn't making any progress at all in getting over the man.

"One condition," he announced.

She hadn't seen him come back. "What's that?"

"You have to smile. I haven't seen that smile of yours in a long time. I watched your interview with Elizabeth Royal, and I thought it was a funeral announcement."

"Oh, really, I didn't think you'd care, Brooks. After all, we haven't spoken to each other for two days, remember?" The words popped out of her mouth before she could stop them, and she wished she had a muzzle. In her mind she imagined she sounded like some jealous high school girl.

Ignoring her contentious words, he merely said, "I want our interview to go well. Let's give it a try. Okay?"

He motioned Mike to his side and gave him a few instructions about camera angles. Brooks didn't care to be reminded about his shoddy treatment of her. He'd flirted outrageously with Katrina and ignored Lindee as much as he could, hoping he could get her to show her true feelings in some display of anger, anything, but it hadn't worked.

Guilt was something new to Brooks. He hadn't had much experience with it, and the shame of what he'd almost brought down upon Lindee had filled him with a sense of anger, at himself mostly, but also at her. As unjustified as it might be, he had been angry with her because he wanted her to have the same confused feelings he had right now. But he knew that was a crazy way to behave, especially since he wanted her as much as ever. She couldn't be dismissed from his mind like all the others in his past. She stuck in his thoughts like glue. And each time he wished her away she came on even stronger than before, filling him with a sad frustration.

For his interview the hard-edged questions from earlier days were gone as he zeroed in to ask about the rigors of campaigning and the challenges it presented on a personal level. He allowed her to spend most of the interview time talking about the difficulty of always being in the public eye. He was cool, calm, and collected, the power of his personality coming through the instant he took the microphone up into his hands. He was a master of this medium, commanding and totally self-assured.

And despite all their problems Lindee owed Brooks one vote of thanks. He'd taught her a lesson about the interview and speechmaking process. A lesson perhaps he wasn't even aware he'd conducted. No matter what the conditions, no matter how difficult or seemingly impossible, she could always find the strength for her public presentations. Somehow, by his own forceful show of strength when he was on camera with her, he'd helped her to enhance her own sense of herself. Aware of Brooks's steady surveillance, she conducted herself with poise and assurance, ready for whatever might come.

When Mike signaled time was almost up Brooks asked his final question: "What will you do, Miss Bradley, if you lose this election?"

Rapid-fire memories of her conversation with her mother came back to her, influencing her answer. "I don't know for sure. I haven't had much time to think about it." She shook her head. "One thing I know is that I'll survive—whatever happens." She smiled into the camera. "But if the polls are right, Mr. Griffin, and I believe they are, I'm not going to have to worry about that. You might try asking Mr. Bullock the same question."

The sweltering lights were switched off and Lindee was relieved. Another interview was over, perhaps her toughest one. Everything about this campaign was suddenly becoming unsatisfactory.

"Thanks, Lindee. I appreciate your agreeing to the interview at the last minute. We'll try to get this on the late night news." Distractedly he wrote himself a note while he talked. "If not, we'll get it on the early morning program."

Their being together should have meant no more to her than it did to him, and his solicitous attitude was just the opposite of what she was feeling. "Anything for publicity, Brooks," she replied with a lighthearted air that was as false as could be.

"Good." He nodded. "And thanks again."

She started to walk away.

"Lindee, wait just a minute." No one was left in the room except the two of them. He stood up. His dark hair glistened in the reflected light and there was a shadow beneath his eyes that gave him a tired look. She could only wonder what he had to say to her.

"Let's try to be kind to each other. Okay? I mean there are only a few more days before the election. I've not been very friendly, I admit, and I apologize, but I can't stand it anymore. If I can't have anything else from you, at least give me your friendship." He held out his hand. "Friends?"

She watched her hand move to his, felt the tingle sweep through her as his warm hand engulfed hers. It was like having a powerful bolt of electricity hit her, but she didn't pull away. Later, she promised herself, she'd sort things out. Right now she'd obeyed her intuition and done the first thing that had come to her mind.

A smile spread along the corners of his mouth. "Let's have a nightcap, shall we? I'm sure your mother wouldn't mind our helping ourselves to her bar."

"I'd like that, Brooks, but I've got a speech to write before I go to bed." Her mind churned in utter confusion. She really would like to be with him. That was the saddest part of this whole unhappy situation.

"Come on, it's raining cats and dogs outside, thundering and lightning. It's a perfect night for two friends to share a night-cap."

As persuasive as he was, she couldn't bring herself to agree to having a drink with him. That was going a little too far, and she'd already taken a big step moments ago. Aware of how easily

138

she'd been subdued by him in the past, she shook her head. "No, thanks. See you on the bus," she said.

Brooks watched her leave, taking in the gentle sway of her hips and the way her hair swung from side to side as she walked. Her fragrance still filled his senses, mocking, tormenting him with the memory of her. He closed his eyes.

There'd been something strange in the way she'd looked at him earlier. It wouldn't do any good for him to try to talk to her about it. She wouldn't acknowledge her feelings aloud, but she'd sent him a message with her eyes. Once she'd met his glance and held it there, and he'd read her look. Lindee cared for him. His heart raced with the thought of it. Her eyes had said she couldn't forget him any more than he could forget her. He felt almost breathless with the knowledge of her unspoken words.

Ever since they'd torn each other apart the other night, he hadn't known what to do with his sadness, and even now he still wasn't certain. The impossibility of the situation between them was disconcerting enough, yet just trying to deal with this complicated woman who'd taken his life by storm was dizzying.

But now he knew, or at least he thought he knew, that she hadn't meant forever when she'd told him to leave her alone. He wanted to rush up the stairs to her bedroom, but he knew he couldn't risk being near her. *Not until this bloody campaign is over,* he thought angrily, and then he told himself he hoped he wouldn't be too late.

"Oh, Lindee." He spoke out into the quiet room. "You and I are meant to be." He laughed then, loud and long, the sound echoing along the walls.

The scheduled trip to the hill country the next day was still on despite the heavy downpour that refused to let up. Weathermen reported record rains all over central and southern Texas. Full of all sorts of assurances, Steve gathered the entire entourage into the center of Vivian's house to wait for the chartered bus to arrive. This was to be the last campaign trip Lindee would make, a quick trip into the fringes of the hill country for an evening speech, a hasty meal, and a late night return. Brooks and his cameraman were there, along with several local reporters and Lindee's campaign staff. Her mother had made arrangements for food and drink to be stored on the bus, enough for an army.

The weather was impossible. Thunder and lightning stormed all around as the rain fell, and it was dark outside, more like night. Yet once the bus started down the highway for the trip, everyone began to have a wonderful time, talking and joking, getting out the food—although they'd just eaten—and suddenly they were having a party. Lindee felt like it, too, and after her conversation with her mother, and the tension between Brooks and herself being eased somewhat last night, she wanted nothing more than to share in the relaxed camaraderie of the group.

She'd been telling herself she had to face up to her emotions—the moods that had been consuming her more and more. Every time she tried to think of how much she resented Brooks's intrusion into her life, a second thought followed that one. Why was she the only one who wasn't ensnared, captivated by his charm? Everywhere she turned she saw signs that something was wrong. The evidence was stacking up in his favor and it confused her.

Lindee felt like some push-me-pull-you toy. One minute she and Brooks were wrapped in each other's arms, the next they'd been caught up in icy frozen silence, and now he wanted to be friends. And he'd been wonderful—kind, attentive, spontaneous. It was insane—the way she was feeling now.

Not knowing what to do or what to think, she helped Earl pass out iced tea, coffee and beer, getting into the group spirit as easily as the rest. A few of the riders sang songs in loud off-key voices while one by one they situated themselves so that they were all sitting in a cluster on the bus, some in the seats, some on top of them, and others on the floor. They were able to make eye contact with one another, and that seemed important for the spirit of the group. Someone began telling a funny story, and soon they were trading off stories and jokes as fast as they could get them out of their mouths.

"Tell them that story you told one time, Brooks," one of the reporters from a San Antonio television station said. "The one about when you were growing up."

Brooks looked quizzical.

"About taking a bath on Saturday night. Most of these people are from the city. They don't know about growing up on a farm."

"Oh, you want to trade off poor stories, is that it?" He grinned. "Well, there's not much story to tell. When I was real little we lived on a dirt tenant farm over in the most primitive part of east Texas. The water came from a pump outside and so we all took turns on Saturday night bathing in a metal washtub in the kitchen. I used to bribe my little brother to let me go first. It was always cleaner that way."

Good-natured laughter filled the bus as he described his outlandish methods of bribery. Lindee watched him as he talked. He wore an open-necked knit shirt in a deep chocolate brown and wheat-colored slacks. His eyes lit up when he talked about his family, and it touched her to hear him speak because his voice was filled with reverence and love.

"It's funny, you know. We didn't think about being poor. Not until we got much older. Old enough to be told by our schoolmates." A flash of pain crossed his face, and then he grinned. "We thought it was wonderful, our life. We always had a garden, a cow, and chickens. We had a real good radio and one day my father brought home an old television set from someplace. I swear the first thing I saw was a newscaster on the screen in a brand new suit, a flashy tie, and a matching grin." He burst into laughter. "Needless to say I wanted to trade places with that guy—right then and there. My brother says if I'd seen Elmer Fudd first I'd have wanted to be a cartoon character."

It was as if the entire group was mesmerized, listening to Brooks talk. They wouldn't let him stop, insisting that he tell them more and more. It wasn't that they didn't know anything about poor families. Everyone in the group probably had someone in their background who'd had at least some of the experiences Brooks talked about, but there was an endearing eloquence

141

in his words and his mannerisms. And they each recognized it for what it was—the touch of love.

"My father extracted one promise from us kids before he died," Brooks said softly. "He made us promise we'd make something of ourselves. Bust your butts, but do it, he said. Every one of us has tried in one way or another."

Engulfed by a sudden sense of compassion that knew no bounds, Lindee fought off the urge to cry. Her memory raced and skittered back to all the times she'd seen other people respond to him. How could she have not understood? How had she missed the entire thing? Blind? She certainly had been that. A shower of despair rained down on her.

How could it be that she'd missed exploring this part of him— the warm, loving, very human side? She watched his eyes, telling herself she hadn't missed it. She'd pushed and shoved and ignored and fought against letting herself have any feelings at all for him. That was why! She'd managed to make him something he wasn't and that had been why she'd been the only one who resisted him. She'd done everything in her power to convince herself he wasn't worth loving. But she'd only been kidding herself.

How could she accuse him of being entirely too ambitious? Of course. Brooks's ambition was no different from hers. They were on the same wavelength. He was satisfying a promise, and she could only wonder how hard he'd had to struggle to get to where he was today.

They were two strong personalities willing to sacrifice, to fight for what they wanted. No, Brooks wanted a future no more than she herself did. The only difference was that he was honest enough to show it—to display his ambitions for all the world to see. And now she knew why. He'd been brought up to believe that it was a good thing—an honest trait to have. She was the one who was at fault. She'd made him something he wasn't, and she'd done it to satisfy her own needs. Brooks never had been the man she'd judged him to be.

She felt a wave of guilt assault her for all the evil thoughts she'd pacified herself with since she'd met him. It had been easier than facing her real emotions, for now she was certain that as preposterous as it was, as much as she'd resisted, it was true. She'd fallen head over heels in love with Brooks Griffin—that outrageous, aggressive, wonderful, intense man. She wanted desperately to reach out and touch him.

Their eyes met and she listened to what her mind silently said. *Come to me, Brooks. Let us be together, our souls, our minds, our bodies linked as one.* She longed to say it aloud, but while her mind was now free, her will was not.

If it weren't for the campaign she could tell him how she felt, and she longed to breach the gap between them. Somehow she had to let him know that she cared for him. If only he'd agree to be there after the election was over. But would he even care how she felt now? No matter. She had to take the chance. She owed it to herself.

CHAPTER EIGHT

"Oh, Miss Bradley, we feel so fortunate that you've come to visit our little community, especially in this terrible weather." The coordinator of the Helotes Committee for Lindee Bradley greeted her and led Lindee into the cloakroom of the old schoolhouse.

Already a large group had gathered and Lindee's entourage from the bus was greeted with such warmhearted enthusiasm that their high spirits merely continued. A photographer who'd traveled with them was snapping pictures of the gaily decorated schoolhouse. Banners of red, white, and blue hung over the doorways and a Texas flag was hung ceremoniously in front of an old pockmarked blackboard. There could be no doubting where they were. The men wore jeans and boots and the women wore denim skirts or jeans themselves. An old fiddler began playing a tune and the crowd responded with clapping and foot-stomping, giving Lindee time to refresh herself before her speech.

Brooks watched Lindee walk slowly across the crowded room. Mike was filming her as she walked over and stood in front of the Texas flag. It made a nice scene, her smiling face outlined in the background by the bright colors of the flag.

She had on a pair of starched jeans and a long-sleeved turquoise blouse with a ruffle around the shoulders. She wore a silver bracelet and a long turquoise necklace, handmade by a friend of hers. There was a glow in her cheeks and a serenity of expression that set the tone for her speech.

Once as she talked she looked at him and smiled, and the look she gave him was an adventure in itself. Her glance reinforced his thoughts. He'd been picking up the vibrations, the change in the tension between them. Ever since he'd interviewed her the other night he'd sensed that subtle shift in her attitude, and it was building stronger and stronger. He'd thought on the bus that the air could have crackled with it as he'd talked directly to her with his eyes.

Brooks knew that having never experienced this feeling before he'd believed it only as a fictional concept, but not any longer. It was true—this magical, mystical connection—this powerful link between the two of them. It was real. He felt it. That was how he knew she felt something special for him. The vibrations were there, rekindled each time their eyes locked. He had to ask her to give him a chance. They had to come to some kind of understanding soon. He couldn't hold back much longer.

Lindee had practiced her speech to perfection and so she gave it, full of conviction and hope, yet able to think her own private thoughts while she spoke. Once she caught Brooks's eye for a moment, and it started her thinking about the multitude of changes she'd passed through in the last several weeks like stepping through so many doors in a funhouse carnival.

She'd gone from a confident, assertive woman to a shaky, unnerved, unsettled creature when Brooks came into her life like some violent cyclone dropped out of a clear sky. Then she'd moved herself into a cool, unruffled existence that seemed more like death than life, accepting the sadness of her situation, forcing herself to go on without him, unable to deal directly with the relationship. It was the worst kind of living. Now it all seemed to clear as she promised herself there was a way. She had to let him know how she felt now. Once the election was over maybe they could begin again, erase the past and find a new beginning.

She finished her speech with a promise. "I promise each of you," she said, "If I'm elected I'll give you the very best commitment, enthusiasm, and the best representation you can have." The applause rocked the room.

"The food's back here," someone called from the buffet line. There was barbecued beef, potato salad, pinto beans, and fresh hot apple pie. As the honored guest Lindee was served first.

Breaking through the crush of people who'd stepped in behind Lindee, Brooks took a great deal of good-natured kidding as he pushed his way to her.

"Lindee, could I talk to you later?" he asked.

She looked at him and a lump grew inside her throat. Now that she'd reconsidered her feelings his masculine scent engulfed her, making her wonder how she could possibly deny him anything. He was by far the most sensual man she'd ever met, and she was at a loss to explain why the knowledge of it always surprised her whenever she was near him.

"Okay, whenever you like," she replied, and looked quickly back at her plate. What was the harm? Every media person on the tour had tried to talk to her.

"Could we eat together?" He made his way back to his rightful place in the line. "Save me a place wherever you sit."

"Okay," she agreed, but it was impossible. Everyone who had braved the storm wanted to shake her hand and say a few words. There was no room for another person what with all the people squeezed in around her.

"Sorry," she offered when Brooks came up later to where she was sitting, but immediately he found himself captured by a group of his own followers. Finishing her meal, Lindee looked over and saw him signing his autograph on napkins.

"Hey, Lindee," Earl called. "I need to talk to you."

"Okay," she said, getting up. "Excuse me, won't you?" she asked the people at her table.

"We've got a problem." Earl was talking to her. Steve, a reporter, and the charter bus driver stood nearby.

"What is it?"

146

"The rain hasn't let up, and there are reports that the roads are flooding."

"How bad is it?"

Earl looked at the driver. "He says he's afraid to try it. That bus is awfully low to the ground."

She sighed, looking out the window. "What do you think we should do?"

Brooks got up from where he was sitting and walked over to them.

"If we can get our group to agree we'll stay here tonight," Earl said. "Our hostess says there's a place just outside of town, a place called Lone Mountain Cabins. It's probably a little rustic, but I think it would be best. We can probably get out of here early in the morning. The storm should have passed by then."

Brooks was listening to Earl's explanation. "I doubt if many of your traveling companions will mind very much," he said. "Look at them."

Earl and Lindee glanced around. True enough, everyone appeared to be having a marvelous time. Their spirited mood hadn't diminished.

Within the hour everyone had been assigned individual cabins after they'd all agreed that staying overnight was the best thing to do. Although it was almost nine o'clock several of Lindee's workers gathered in Earl's cabin, reviewing the evening's events. Steve had been in touch with campaign headquarters where the latest results of a straw poll were expected. Their hopes were high because Lindee had gained six additional points since they'd taken the last poll. As time went on and communications were shut down because of the storm, their attentions turned to the last day prior to the election. It was agreed that the best strategy for the final day would be to travel through San Antonio going door to door asking the voters to cast their ballot for Lindee. They also agreed they should hope for sunshine.

Lindee said her good-nights and walked down the dirt path that was now muddy. Her cabin was away from the others, and she took down her umbrella and let the rain fall gently across her until she was soaked. It was a way of releasing tension, and she knew she needed to be as relaxed as possible for the next forty-eight hours. Her spontaneous action made her feel like a little girl again, and she loved the sensation of the rainwater slowly sliding down her body, leaving no part of her untouched.

Standing on the wooden porch of the cabin he shared with Mike, Brooks watched her in the pale evening light. He saw her close the umbrella and twirl around once, letting the rain soak her to the skin. He knew she was smiling although he couldn't see her face clearly. The sight of her there made him ache with longing. He had to talk to her.

The dark mountain peaks Lindee could see in the distance made the chilly night air seem even cooler. Opening the door to her cabin she smelled the rich scent of cedar wood floating in the air from someone's fireplace. With delight she discovered she had a fireplace of her own and the wood and matches had been stacked conveniently nearby.

It seemed so romantic a night that she didn't think the cabin was nearly as rustic as Earl had envisioned. The living area was enchanting, with old scarred hardwood floors covered with occasional throw rugs, a faded green sofa and a chair that had matched at one time but had long since faded to a mottled brown color. The stone fireplace covered one entire wall and in front of it was a multicolored rag rug that someone had probably lovingly sewn together. Mindless of how late it was, she quickly started a fire. Now her frolic in the rain seemed distant and she felt cold. The thought of sleeping by the fireplace enticed her.

Lindee stood staring down at the fire, watching it catch and spread along the logs in marching flame. Ever since Brooks had said he wanted to talk to her she'd tried to guess what it was he wanted to say, and the fact that he hadn't found a way to talk to her only made her more curious. Whatever it was, she knew she desperately wanted to be able to bring herself to tell him that she cared for him. Somehow she had to find the courage, and she only had one day in which to do it. If she waited until after the election it might be too late.

She picked up two cushions from the couch and arranged them on top of the rag rug so that she could lean against them, but first she had to get out of her wet clothes. She began to unbutton the cotton blouse that clung to her like a second skin. Goosebumps ran along her arms and she struggled with the difficult buttons. When she finally had it unbuttoned and was peeling it off she ran into the tiny bedroom and scooped up the two quilts she'd seen at the foot of the bed. Returning to the living room, she spread one of the quilts out neatly across the rag rug. As quickly as she could she took off the rest of her clothes and draped them over the edge of the rock fireplace to dry. She wrapped herself up in the remaining quilt and stood before the fire, letting the quilt warm her back, opening it so that the heat of the flame could warm the front of her body. She was chilled to the bone.

A light tapping at her door stunned her for a moment, and she stood where she was, unable to respond. When the tapping persisted she covered herself with the quilt bunched up around her shoulders and walked across the cool hardwood floors in her bare feet.

"Who is it?" she whispered through the door, feeling slightly foolish when she thought of what she must look like.

"It's Brooks. Listen, it's important that I talk to you for just a moment, please."

Every nerve in her body was sending out warning signals, her face felt flush, and her ears were filled with a roaring sensation. She knew she was taking a terrible chance, especially when her mood was so vulnerable, and yet she had to know if there was anything that could be salvaged between them.

"For a minute," she answered apprehensively. She unlocked the flimsy wooden door.

"I saw the smoke coming from your chimney and I thought you might still be up." He stepped inside and glanced back from where he'd come. "Everyone else has gone to bed."

She could smell the dampness of the night mix with the faint musty tracings of his after-shave. Aware of her bare body beneath the quilt and the warm stirrings he was able to awaken in her without even trying, she told herself to be as quick with her words as she could be. As a precaution she looked outside for herself, but the night was dark. "You can't stay, Brooks."

"Just ten minutes. I just want to tell you something." He watched her eyes then and chuckled. "I'm lying. Of course I want to stay, but only long enough to tell you what I came to say." He walked over to the fireplace where the fire had built up to perfection.

"I have something to tell you, too, or at least to talk to you about." She closed the door and followed him.

He turned and leaned back against the wooden mantel, staring intently into her eyes. "I don't know quite where to start. You told me to stay away from you, that you wanted nothing more to do with me. I was hurt and angry. I wanted you to hurt, too, Lindee, and I didn't understand for a long time why I felt so guilty, so full of shame. I think I do now."

She didn't know what she'd expected to hear, but an admission of guilt hadn't been it. Shakily she sat down on the quilt.

He sat down next to her, his legs crossed, facing her. "I'm jumping from one thought to the next like some errant tennis ball, but I'll get out what I want to say if you'll just hang on." He longed to touch her and once he reached out to feel her damp hair, but she pulled back and so he let his hand fall to his knee. "Whatever you felt for me before has changed in the last few days. I can feel it."

She looked surprised.

"Not overtly, never that. You're too cool a lady for that. But I could just feel it, Lindee. Your attitude toward me has changed, and I wanted to talk to you before the election. I couldn't leave this silence hanging between us another second and I decided it was now or never when I saw you walking in the rain earlier."

She held the quilt to her in a tight fist, suddenly reminded of her nudity. "How could you feel this change, Brooks?"

"I don't know. I saw it in your eyes, I think. Don't you believe that a couple who care for each other very deeply have a certain sense about them?"

"Care for each other very deeply?" she echoed questioningly.

"Lindee, you've got to promise me that there'll be a future for us once the election is over. You must give me the chance to prove to you that I'm not as terrible as you think," he continued, his voice full of touching desperation.

"I never intended to put you in a situation that could cause you any difficulties with your campaign. Honestly. I've been guilty of the worst case of selfishness in the history of man. I'll admit to that, but I've never done anything intentionally to hurt you."

Mesmerized by his words and the forceful way he spoke, she didn't interrupt. It was too touching listening to him pour out his feelings for her.

"Except that night with Katrina. I'll admit I was so hurt that I only wanted to strike back at you." Shaking his head, he grinned. "See, I told you I was talking all around everything."

She smiled softly at him. She'd never seen him so disorganized in his conversation, so ill at ease with his own words. Gone was the man who had the power to control a microphone or an audience, replaced by a man who was talking nonstop, going from one sequence of events to another, clearly distraught.

"Okay, let me start over again. When you and I first met I was curious about you, interested in watching you take on Bullock, sort of like watching David and Goliath. Then something happened and I couldn't concentrate on anything else but you. I was like a man gone mad. We had our television interview and I found that I really enjoyed our bantering conversation. You're a very brilliant lady, and I'm discovering more and more each day just how bright you are. When I kissed you I enjoyed it, but I told myself that it wasn't unusual to feel attracted to a striking lady like you."

He reached out and took her hand in his, and this time she didn't resist. She wanted to cry as she listened to him pour out his heart to her. Oh, God, how could she have ever doubted this sensitive, wonderful man? His hand was warm and firm when she tenderly let her thumb run against his skin.

"I guess it was the night that you fell into the splashing fountain that did it. When you fell I couldn't wait to see what you'd do, how you'd react, and when you did what you did I loved it. It was perfect."

They both laughed. "Am I having any effect on you, Lindee? Do you see what I'm trying to say to you? Shhh," he said, and reached a finger up to her lips before she could reply. "Don't answer me yet. Hear me out.

"And then when I found you in the hot tub, I was only thinking of my needs and how much I wanted you. Nothing of what you said seemed real to me. I wanted you, and I was determined to have you. Nothing could have stopped me. Oh, Lindee." He sighed. "When I came to your room that night, it was magic. I thought it was the most wonderful thing I'd ever experienced, and it went a lot deeper than just making love to you. I felt, for the first time in my life . . . I felt as though I were in communion with another soul. I can't describe how much that night meant to me."

"Me too," she said softly.

"You mean that?" he asked in a voice full of doubt. He wanted so badly to take her in his arms then. It was the most natural of feelings, but he was afraid he'd frighten her away, and she'd make him leave before he'd finished what he had come to say.

She nodded her head and remained very still. If he kisses me, I'm gone, she thought, and briefly wondered how long he'd been there. The rain pounded on the roof and flashes of lightning echoed from far away. Every now and then an ember crackled in the fireplace, and Lindee wished she could hold onto this moment forever.

"But, see, when you told me off that night on the river, I couldn't believe it. I was like a crazed fiend, totally knocked away by what you were telling me. It was as if you didn't care for me, as though that night had meant nothing to you at all. And that hurt." The cadence in his speech changed, revealing even more of his raw emotions. "That was why I came after you that night, waiting for you at your house. And then when I saw how much I'd hurt you it hit me. Suddenly like a shot in the night everything was clear, and I felt terrible. You were right, and I was wrong. I hated myself for what I'd put you through." He took a deep breath. "And I have to admit that I hated you a little then, too, because I thought I was hurting and you weren't. That's why I acted like such a fool with Katrina."

She couldn't hold her tongue. "But I *was* hurting, Brooks. You'll never know how much. I thought I'd lost you, and all the time I was trying to tell myself how bad you were, my heart kept insisting that I loved you."

"Loved me? Lindee, do you love me?" he demanded.

Her answer was simply "Yes."

He couldn't help himself. He reached out and brought her face toward his until they were less than an inch apart. "I love you," he murmured, and kissed her with the tenderest of kisses, letting his warm lips describe his desire, and then he let her go and leaned back against one of the cushions, staring into the fire as if it held a message for him.

"This is the most wonderful night of my life, Lindee. And I've got so many things to say to you, to tell you about."

She felt all warm inside from his words and his kiss. Leaning back against the arm of the couch she listened to him, watching how the firelight changed the color of his eyes like a kaleidoscope, aware of how his hand was trailing across the edge of the quilt that kept her hidden from him. She thought her heart would burst with the joy of it all.

He started to talk again, unable to stop himself, he was so full of pent-up emotion. "I want you to know all about me."

"For a frame of reference?"

He looked at her, trying to gauge her emotions, hoping that they were the same as his. "Do you really love me?"

"I said I did." She laughed.

"Well then, that's why I want you to know me. It's more than a frame of reference. I want each of us to know everything there is to know about the other so that we can share what's really important to us." He stretched out his arm as far as it would reach to play with a wisp of her hair. Softly he said, "But that won't ever happen. Not completely."

"Oh?" She leaned her cheek against his hand. "Why?"

"Because you're too complex a woman, and I think the real you is always willing to grow, to change. I don't think I'll ever know you, really know you."

"That's funny, Brooks, because I have always considered you the more complex of the two of us. You're the one always thinking, challenging yourself and others, moving ahead with resolution to get whatever it is you're after."

"That, my dear Lindee, sounds almost like one of your accusations again about my ambition, but I'll ignore it." He watched her shake her head in denial. "Good, because that reminds me of something I want to tell you about me. The major networks are looking me over. The woman from CBS who interviewed you was with her news director, and they talked to me for a little while. There's no job offer yet, not from any network. I hear ABC might be interested, too, but there's nothing definite."

She could hear the pride as he spoke. "Oh, Brooks, that's wonderful news. It's just what you've been hoping for."

"Yeah." He grinned and looked back at the flames. "If I could just do something really big like breaking a story, maybe get hold of some undercover investigative news or something. I could be sure of getting what I've always wanted if I did that. Anyway"— he sighed—"I haven't been able to think of anything yet. I've been too busy thinking about you."

They talked on and on, so wrapped up in each other it was as if they were all alone in the world. Nothing could break their concentration now. Together, for the first time in their lives they were discovering firsthand the miracle of love, and it was as absorbingly dramatic as the opening of a rosebud. Nothing else held any meaning for them.

Finally Brooks looked deeply into her eyes. "We've ignored one thing, Lindee. The issue of commitment between us. I've already made up my mind. I want to marry you. Now I want you to take your time deciding. I don't want an answer until after the election. That way you don't have any pre-election obligations."

She started to speak.

"No." He took her hand and put it to his lips. "Don't say anything. Just trust me. I'll be there waiting for your answer after this is all over." Tenderly he took her fingertips one by one and kissed them, and then he moved nearer to her, until they were so close she could feel the heat of him.

Brooks didn't speak, although his eyes did, and his lips as he kissed her gently on her eyelids, the tip of her nose, and then her mouth. And she was lost. There was no use in letting her mind try to convince her emotions that it was wrong because it wasn't.

What they'd pronounced with their words remained now to be satisfied through their physical union, and as they touched, nothing could have separated them then. This was the commitment they'd each longed for.

"I hope to God that we're not found out, Brooks, because we can't stop now." Even as she spoke Lindee felt her body fill with passionate arousal as he unclenched her fist from the quilt and let it fall from her shoulders.

His body responded to the raw vein of passion in her voice and a wild surge of desire passed through him. "Don't worry," he whispered before reaching out to her once more. "We're safe. I made sure Mike was asleep before I came. No one knows I'm here." His confidence had returned when she'd admitted that she loved him, and now he knew only that he wanted her more than anything he'd ever wanted in his life. A shudder ran through him when he felt her body respond instinctively to his touch, and he heard her breath become shallow and quicken.

It was as it was meant to be and there was no resistance, no denial as they came together in the darkness. Brooks pulled her into his arms and kissed her mouth with tender greeting, which soon turned to urgent desire as she returned his kiss with all the love she'd stowed away for so long. She could feel his heart

155

pounding so close to her own, and her pulse quickened so she thought she couldn't bear it.

Then he pulled slightly away as he reached for the top button of his shirt; but she had her own ideas, and she threw back her head and reached out, undressing him herself with quick, steady movements while he brought his warm mouth down to her breasts, kissing one and then the other, arousing them with his tongue in teasing torment, feeling her body move nearer in ardent response.

With her help at last he shrugged off the remainder of his clothes. The light touch of her hands had set every nerve in his body on fire, and he pulled her to him in agonizing haste.

Then they lay down together across the quilt, each watching the way the fire flickered across their bodies, casting the light this way and that. Wordlessly they began a slow discovery of each other, first with their eyes and then with their lips, stretching out against each other, savoring each look, each caress as if it might be their last.

Lindee sought out the pulse point of his throat and softly kissed it, then brought her lips down to his chest, sending tiny kisses along his frame to his ribs and then to where his waist began, before moving along his quivering stomach. Brooks let his kisses fall along the tenderest parts of her, from the lobe of her ear to the delicate flesh of her arms and then down her body, allowing his lips to linger along his inner thigh where the maddening sensation drove her to moan aloud in unmitigated desire. Then his lips moved back up along her hip, her stomach, and on until he was once again covering her nipple with his wet mouth. His lips were magic and she knew only that they needed each other, needed to let their bodies speak.

He moved up over her, and she gripped him to her, wanting nothing more than to feel his body pressed against hers. She brought his lips to hers and kissed him with a fervor that knew no bounds, running her fingers through his hair and then down along his shoulders and back until she touched the beginning line of his buttocks. She began a slow tracing of his soft flesh with her hands while her body was arching up to his, and he reached beneath her, scooping her up to meet his demanding thrusts. And then her hands were firm and strong, running up and down his body in total abandon as she responded to the force that was in control of her.

She gave herself willingly to him as their rhythms met and joined, pulsating together faster and faster, building higher and higher until she was lost in that special place that has no name. "Brooks," she cried, and knew he could not hear her as his body had stiffened in glorious passion.

CHAPTER NINE

In the wee hours of the morning, just before the sky became light, Brooks threw on his slacks, quickly stepped into his shoes, and carrying his shirt and socks in his hand, left Lindee's cabin. The night had been as extraordinary as they had imagined it would be . . . a magical rapture that neither of them had ever known existed.

With loving fingers she'd tried to smooth down his hair before he left but each time she tried he'd bring her into his arms for one final embrace. Laughingly she gave up and watched him go stealthily out the door, looking like some little lost boy as he dashed to his own cabin.

The fire had died down, leaving in its wake a pile of glowing ashes that warmed the room. His presence still spoke to her from every shadow, every board, every piece of furniture. Lindee remembered their night together as an unbelievable happening, a blending and igniting of two souls becoming one.

She stoked the ashes, exposing a red ember still alive. Lying down, she rolled over on her back on the quilt and smiled as she remembered his long, haunting kisses that had spoken of gentleness and made her body long to respond to him over and over again.

There was no guilt, no sense of shame over what had occurred. Not now. Being with Brooks had been the most natural thing she could have done, and she was glad they'd shared their feelings in the way they had. But she couldn't dismiss the nagging threat that made her swallow hard when it came to mind that if someone had seen them together the election would be lost.

And yet what they had shared had been too beautiful to be displaced by guilt. Now she was going to miss Brooks, she knew. Mike had made arrangements for Brooks and himself to be driven to Houston this morning. They had to get to the television station to prepare for election night, Brooks had explained, and he was taking with him the film Mike had shot of her speech last night. But with a lingering kiss Brooks had promised to be with her as soon as he could, hopefully the morning after the election.

Three hours later a knock sounded at the cabin door. Groggy with sleep, she stumbled up, wrapped her quilt around her, and went to answer it.

"Good morning." Earl smiled. "I trust you slept well. The bus is leaving in about twenty minutes. We've got hot coffee and fresh doughnuts to go."

"Mmmm," she replied, thick-tongued. "Fresh doughnuts?"

"You have some followers who also happen to be excellent cooks. Lucky you."

"Yes, lucky me." She smiled, sure that she'd never doubt her good fortune again.

The rain had disappeared and they both looked at the clear sky gratefully. Earl spoke up. "Get yourself dressed and meet us at the bus. We'll be in San Antonio before nine this morning. There's still a lot of handshaking to do before nightfall."

The bus ride proved to be much quieter than the day before. Lindee spent most of the trip trying to sleep, but each time she closed her eyes Brooks's face loomed before her, that eager boyish grin of his taking control of her thoughts, pushing the idea of sleep far, far away from the center of her mind.

When they were entering the San Antonio city limits the bus

driver pulled over to the side of the road. Lindee watched along with the others as Earl and Steve got off the bus to meet a man who'd flagged them down. She recognized him as one of their campaign workers who'd remained in San Antonio while they'd made their trip. Young, eager to please, he had turned into a first-rate gofer, and Steve had often commented on his helpfulness.

"What was it?" Lindee asked Earl when he got back on the bus.

"Nothing. We'll talk about it later," he replied tersely.

But she could tell from the ashen look of his face that whatever the news, it wasn't good. Steve walked hastily past her, all the way to the back of the bus, where he sat down alone.

"Earl?" she asked. "What is it?" She patted the empty bus seat next to her, urging him to sit down.

"I'd rather wait till we get home, Lindee," he said.

She could see beads of perspiration on his face and it frightened her. Anxiously she pushed her point. "Is it my mother? Tell me, Earl. I can take it, but I want you to tell me right now." The more she looked at him the more certain she was that the news was terrible.

"No, Lindee, it's not your mother." He glanced over at her then and yet when their eyes met he quickly turned his head away.

"Please," she insisted.

"It's about the election," he said at last.

"Oh, well, it can't be as bad as all that. You look like you might have a heart attack or something." She grinned playfully at him. "Don't scare me like that again, Earl. You wouldn't believe all the tragic things I was imagining."

"Well, Lindee, this is pretty bad." His voice was ragged with emotion. "Ted Bullock just announced on all the television stations and the radio that he'd received a group of pictures of a man leaving your cabin in the middle of the night last evening with only part of his clothes on. Bullock supposedly has also shown the newspeople a picture of you kissing the mystery man

160

good-bye with only a blanket or something partially covering you."

She gasped.

"That damned man is playing it for all he's worth, trying to make you out as undeserving of the honor of being a state senator. He's grandstanding his shock and dismay all over the state as fast as the news can travel."

She felt only shock as she listened to him talk on and on, barely keeping his voice to a whisper. Sitting frozen in the seat, she wasn't aware of the tears that ran silently down her cheeks or that she held her hands tightly clasped together, as if she were helplessly trying to keep herself from screaming out.

"Texas is one of the most conservative states in the union." Earl sighed. "I don't know exactly what we can do to try to counterattack. It's probably too late, but as soon as we get back we'll sit down and try to think this thing through." He drew in his breath. "I'll be willing to bet you've been right all along, Lindee. Brooks was a part of this. He had to be or maybe it was Mike. Oh, hell, I don't know who it was, but I'll guarantee you one thing. When I find the son of a gun who did this I'm going to punch him out."

Her throat felt tight and restricted. She fought for breath. "Are you sure they don't know who the man was, Earl?"

"The pictures were taken with an infrared lens on a Nikon camera. An expert did it. And whoever you were with, Lindee, was lucky; either lucky or a very careful planner. Only his back was seen in any of the pictures. The only full-face view was of you."

He reached out for her hand, and when she didn't give it to him he took it anyway, covering it up with his own clammy one. He looked sick as they rode in silence toward her mother's house.

"Have the driver take me to my home, Earl." Her voice was forlorn, like a little child's, wavering between trying to stay strong and wanting to cry out. "We're going to lose, aren't we?" she asked after he'd given the driver the address.

A squeeze of his hand was his answer.

She fought off choking panic as the events became more and more real to her. "I'm so sorry, Earl. So sorry."

"Aren't we all?"

When the bus pulled up in front of Lindee's home there were photographers and cameramen stationed outside on the lawn, looking too much like vultures about to take their meal. Earl and Steve formed a two-man barricade on either side of her to keep her away from the newspeople. Once inside the door they made sure it was locked behind them and all three began pulling down the blinds as quickly as they could.

Lindee had managed to hold a tight rein over her emotions, but she was beginning to feel the break coming once she reached the safety of her own home. She'd shut her mind like a steel trap, not allowing herself to think, but now her mind was beginning to race away.

"I'm going to call your mother, Lindee. She was expecting you to show up at her house. Vivian will probably want to come over. What should I tell her?"

Lindee shook her head. She stood on the first step of the stairway that led to the bedrooms. Already her body was starting to shake like the first tremors of an earthquake, and she knew she had to get away.

"She'll probably want to come anyway. You know Vivian." Earl watched her carefully for a few seconds. "Are you going to be okay?"

Not trusting herself to speak, Lindee merely nodded twice.

"Steve and I are going to work up a statement. I'll give it to the press so maybe they'll leave us and go away."

Lindee started up the stairs and then turned back. In a voice full of unshed tears she whispered, "Earl, why do you think it was Brooks? Why did you mention him first?" She had to know.

Earl fidgeted with the telephone cord before he looked at her. "Because, Lindee, he and his cameraman had a bag full of photographic equipment when they got off the bus. I saw them carrying it all off in the rain. Steve has been through all the other people's bags on board the bus. There was no infrared lens in any of them. Whoever took the pictures got them out of the place in a hurry. Brooks and his cameraman were gone before sunup. He didn't tell me he was leaving. Did he tell you?" He sighed unhappily. "And how was it that Bullock was the one to expose the pictures? Somebody gave them to him. Someone who wanted him to win. Remember what you told me before about Brooks? It had to be him. There couldn't be anyone else."

She walked up the stairs, her legs weak and shaky. The tears had begun again and this time she didn't even try to stop them. What good would it do?

Her house was small compared to her mother's—a two-story cottage set into the hills with a magnificent view of the city and a summer breeze that defied the Texas heat. She loved it here. There was something quiet and placid about the place and she'd filled it with a lifetime of antique treasures. It was here that she'd come to let herself open up.

Here, all alone, she sat, first in utter silence, letting the tears run like rain, trailing over her cheeks to drop from her chin down onto her lap, soaking her clothes. For a long time she remained that way, unaware of anything, devoid of any thoughts, full of a pain that knew no bounds.

And then she heard noises, a deep bewildering sound, more like a wounded animal than anything human. Startled, she jumped up from where she was sitting, ran to the door, and made certain it was locked. No intruders would be allowed to interfere with her grief. She wouldn't permit it. But after a moment she realized the sounds were her own. She fell to the floor, her sobs deep, wracking, filling her with the only consolation she could find right now—her own expression of pain. She let the bitter tears flood without restraint.

And every time she thought of facing what had happened she cringed. She wanted to crawl up into her bed, snuggle down into her warm comforter, and hide, not to come out until someone could assure her this had been only a terribly frightening nightmare.

Brooks had betrayed her in the most damning of ways. Her deepest fears were coming true, bringing with them the downfall of her life. He had taken her life up in his hands, brushed aside her doubts, captured her love, brought her passion to new heights, and made everything happen just as he'd wanted. He'd reached out and wrapped his hand around to take hold of her heart, and then he hadn't simply discarded it, he'd devastated it. And as if to say to her that his betrayal of her love wasn't enough, he'd made doubly certain she was ruined. He'd taken the election away, and maybe her political career.

She didn't know how long she stayed where she was, stretched out across the floor, so caught up in her anguish that she didn't know where she was and didn't care. After she'd run out of tears she turned over and stretched out on the floor, listening to the dry sobs that shook her body from time to time, thinking about Brooks and what he'd done.

Like the good lawyer she was she began to recount what had happened between them. From the first time she'd met him he'd given her the impression that he didn't like her, and she'd heard more than once about his wanting Bullock to win. She remembered how he'd interrupted her press conference the second day he'd come on her campaign trail, how he'd yawned noisily, distracting the audience when she'd been making her important fund-raising speech in Fort Worth, and then how he'd set it up so she looked as though kissing old men was her trade.

It was all coming together, she thought. She could convince any jury in the land of his guilt. The facts were all in. Guilty as charged.

Carefully she recalled the day he'd interviewed her out on the terrace of her hotel room, going for the jugular with his insinuations and his abrupt challenges. If she hadn't been so well prepared he could have ruined her then. The night he'd made her stumble and fall into the water fountain must have been what made him change his approach. Even as she was being made to look foolishly ridiculous she'd managed to steal his thunder by tripping him, sending him into the water with her. And so he'd decided on another tactic. If he couldn't publicly damage her quickly enough with his disruptions and his insulting interviewing techniques he'd try to seduce her. That had proven his smartest move, she thought, and felt a new tear begin to trickle down her face.

He'd done an excellent job of that, ignoring her resistance, making her think she was special, doing everything in his power to prove what a virile man he was, and then finally when all else hadn't quite succeeded he'd told her he loved her. His admission of love had sealed her response and he must have known that was the only thing that would make her throw caution to the wind. He'd set her up. Probably laughing about it as he worked with the cameraman, trying to figure out how to make certain his face was never revealed. She hated that lying man with every part of her being. Just as she had warned herself he'd do, Brooks had remained protected and she'd lost everything. A tiny voice reminded her that she had played a part in it, too, but there was absolutely no way she could allow herself to think about what she'd done. She simply couldn't bear it. The wound was too fresh.

"Lindee." Vivian knocked at her door. "Please, darling, may I come in? I don't want to disturb you, dear, but just let me talk to you for a moment."

She hadn't heard her mother come up the stairs. She hadn't heard anything in a long time, only her own voice. Feeling the aching puffiness around her eyes, Lindee stood up. She was a strong woman, she told herself, and she'd need every bit of her strength and courage to do what she had to do.

Walking quickly to the bathroom, she readjusted her blouse and looked in dismay at her wet skirt. She ran cool water in the sink and took a washcloth out of the linen closet, soaked it in the water, wrung it out, and began wiping her eyes with it.

"I'm coming," she called back at last. "Just give me a minute." She couldn't stand to have her mother see her looking so bad, and hastily she took off her clothes and threw a silk caftan over

165

her. Then she walked over and unlocked the door, dreading it with all her soul.

"Darling, you don't have to talk or say anything to me. I just had to make certain you were all right." Vivian entered the room, carefully avoiding eye contact with Lindee. She walked over to the window and looked out. "The reporters are leaving now. Earl has issued a statement and told them they wouldn't be able to see you today."

Lindee gritted her teeth, drew herself up to her full height, and spoke, hesitantly at first and then more and more smoothly. "Mother, I want to ask your forgiveness. I'm so terribly sorry about all this."

Her mother turned with a sharp twist of her body. "Stop that. You owe me nothing. I told you that before, or at least I tried to. You happened to have made a mistake."

Lindee sucked in her breath.

"A mistake in timing, dear. That's all. And you let yourself forget that you were a public figure. It's a mistake easily made." Vivian sat down on the bed and motioned for Lindee to sit next to her. "It was Brooks Griffin, wasn't it?"

Tears welled in Lindee's eyes again, tears she didn't know she had left. She looked her mother full in the face. "Yes."

"I figured as much," Vivian replied. She reached out and let her fingers interweave with her daughter's. "Well, Lindee, don't feel you have to apologize to me. Remember what I told you before. Love is all that matters."

The pain ran through her with a fresh thrust. Vivian thought Lindee and Brooks were in love.

"But it's not . . . it's not. Brooks set me up, Mother. And now I've thrown away everything, hurt you, hurt Earl. I'm so full of shame I could just die."

The sobs built up again and Vivian pulled Lindee into her arms and let her cry. "I told you I love you. Earl will get over it. He doesn't look as if he's taking it quite as hard as you think." She patted Lindee's back. "If I didn't know better I'd think he was trying to work on a strategy for the future. If I didn't know better, that is."

"What am I going to do, Mother?"

Vivian lifted her daughter's face in her hands. "You are a Bradley. You're a fighter. A hardheaded one at that. And you have been ever since you were a little slip of a girl. I don't know what you're going to do, but I'll help you." She kissed her on the forehead. "The first step is always the hardest."

She left Lindee alone then and went downstairs, promising to fix a lunch fit for a queen. She'd made Lindee promise she'd come down to eat later. Alone once more, Lindee replayed her mother's words over in her head, telling herself she couldn't hide away like some errant child. An idea formed in her mind after a while and she got up and went to her closet. She pulled out fresh clothes and her most comfortable walking shoes.

When her mother called up the stairway later telling her lunch was ready, Lindee closed her eyes pensively for a long time before striding purposefully down the stairs. Hearing voices in the living room she went in there first. Earl, Steve, and a handful of her staff were there, watching the noon news.

Remaining silent she stood in the doorway and saw firsthand the pictures that had been taken of her. It was the ultimate humiliation. It was also a mental reminder that Earl was right. Brooks was responsible. If he hadn't been, he would have called her, found some way to contact her in her time of need. She wanted to break down and cry again but she told herself there wasn't any time. She'd have to save her tears.

"Well," she said, and everyone in the room looked at her with surprise. "Remind me to buy one of those cameras, Earl. I may need it sometime."

Nobody quite knew whether to laugh or remain quiet, and so they sat stoically staring ahead. Lindee went over and stood in front of the television.

She cleared her throat, mentally calling on herself for all the inner strength she could muster. "I want to say to each of you, from the bottom of my heart, how terribly sorry I am. I'm sorry that I've asked you to give so much of yourselves—your time, your energies—to my campaign, and then I've let you down like this. I know this will cost me the election. Bullock will see to it, with the help of his friends. And I know how much this election meant to you. I've let you down and I'm terribly ashamed."

Earl started to speak.

"Wait." She raised her hand. "Let me finish. I can't do anything about this now. I've made the mistake and it can't be erased. No amount of apologizing or agonizing over my guilt is going to take that away. But I'll tell you what I am going to do." She paused. "I'm going out into San Antonio this afternoon and I'm going to campaign like hell."

It was clear from their facial expressions that they had expected to hear anything but what she had said to them. Taking time to let themselves understand what she said, almost in unison they stood up, each wanting to say something to her, their faces full of admiration.

"I'm going to have lunch first," she said with a faint smile. "You're all welcome to eat with us, and then to finish off this campaign just as we'd planned." She looked each of them in the eye, one by one. "And if you want to leave right now I wouldn't blame you a bit. I just hope you'll take my apology with you."

"I'm starving," Earl said, and everyone laughed. En masse they entered the dining room, talking and laughing like old times.

Vivian had arranged a buffet with several cold salads, rolls, and iced tea. She came out from the kitchen. "I'm going to have to go and get my good walking shoes if we're going to cover a lot of territory this afternoon."

"Well, you'd better, Mother, because we're going to cover a great deal of territory before we call it a day." Lindee laughed and so did everyone else. It was the first time she'd felt like laughing since early this morning. Was it a sign that she was going to make it? She didn't know right now. She just had to keep busy; keep busy and try not to think.

As they prepared to leave, Vivian pulled Lindee back into a

corner of the kitchen away from everyone else. "Maybe this isn't the time to talk about this, darling, but I felt like I just had to say it. I think you shouldn't make up your mind so quickly about Brooks."

"Oh, please, Mother, please," Lindee begged, her eyes swimming with tears again.

"I know, I know what you're thinking," Vivian admitted. "And I'm just a silly old woman, but you'll have to admit, dear, that I've been a good judge of character for a good number of years."

Wiping her eyes, Lindee got out her sunglasses. Her eyes were still swollen from all her crying, and things didn't seem to be improving. "You don't know all the circumstances, Mother, believe me. And I don't have time to tell you about it now, but I will, and when I do you'll change your mind about Brooks Griffin."

Within ten minutes they'd formed a caravan of cars and driven into town, Steve in the lead car. He was the one who'd mapped out where they'd start and how they'd go door to door. A few media people followed them, but no one would comment or answer any of their questions, and so they finally left Lindee alone.

Once she began she found that it became easier and easier. She let herself concentrate on the people, listening to their problems and their concerns. And when she couldn't concentrate she moved in a haze, fighting the demons in her mind, blurring out painful thoughts. Fortunately, no one mentioned the allegations against her—probably because they were too embarrassed. All the citizens she spoke with were polite.

After a couple of hours had passed Lindee found herself on a street all alone, having left the others behind. She was caught up in it now, campaigning like a vengeful force—pouring her energy into it with everything she had to give—doing anything, trying not to think. And it was late in the evening before she stopped, too exhausted to go on.

They returned to her house. Earl unlocked the door for her,

insisting on checking out her house for any media types lurking around, while her mother tried to talk her into going to her home. At her insistence Lindee finally convinced them that all she wanted was to be left alone for a while. There would be no one with her tonight, and she was relieved and sad, all at the same time.

When they'd finally gone Lindee walked aimlessly through the house. It was chilly outside and she thought of starting a fire, but changed her mind. Exhaustion enveloped her, and she turned out the downstairs lights and went slowly up the stairs.

Tired and dirty she turned on the shower, letting the warm water hit her body everywhere, tingling her flesh back to life. She washed her hair, too, and it wasn't until she was reaching for the fluffy towel that she realized she was crying again—warm, silent tears that stung her already hurting eyes even more.

She put on a silk gown and got into the bed. Then she groaned and got up again and went into the bathroom for Kleenex. Once she returned she lay there letting her mind replay all the events that had led up to Brooks's final betrayal.

She'd considered him a master of his craft, admiring his amazing ability to command a television audience's attention with just the play of his words. But she hadn't known that he was a master of other things also. A master of deceit.

Shutting her eyes, she curled up into a ball and sank farther down into the bed. How could she have done this to herself? That was the ultimate question—the one she'd avoided asking herself all day long. Brooks followed his conscience, did what he wanted to do for his own gains. What was her excuse? No matter how much Lindee wanted to hold Brooks totally responsible, she knew she couldn't.

Putting the entire blame on him was wrong, and yet she'd let herself carry out the mental charade all day long because it was far easier than dealing with the real issue head on. Brooks had asked to come in for ten minutes. She'd given him the night.

He might be a liar, and a schemer, and too dangerously ambitious, but she had known it all along, and still she'd let herself succumb to his charm and his mystique. Every time she could remember being near him she'd heard a voice deep inside warning her of his cunning ways. Yet time and time again she'd dismissed her fears and finally she'd convinced herself, after watching his actions, that her doubts were ridiculous.

She'd even gone so far as to tell herself last night to follow her instincts! Impulses were more like it. She'd responded to a handsome man, a romantic setting, a sexual tension, a mysterious attraction and the seductive words "I love you." And now she was responding to a grief so profound she didn't know if she could bear it.

"Why on earth didn't I kick him out?" she shouted to the four walls. "Why did I ever let him stay? Ten minutes. That's all he asked for, and I gave him the entire night." Her screams became a plaintive wail.

Alone at last, she could admit that his betrayal had broken her heart. She waited for some signal that it was destroyed—some noise of a cracking down the middle, blood, death—whatever was supposed to come because of a broken heart. And for that Brooks was the one responsible. She could only wonder if she'd survive it.

When election day came and went, taking with it the laurels to the winner, Ted Bullock, she wondered if indeed this second humiliation would be the final break. Bitterly she told herself she had an entire cast to thank for her loss—Ted Bullock, Brooks Griffin, and last, but not least, Lindee Bradley. She didn't even bother to turn on the television set. Earl had to be the bearer of the final news.

Bullock had retained his seat in the senate by defeating Lindee, all right. But it wasn't fair. She knew it, he knew it, and wherever Brooks was, he knew it too. The fact that she had lost only by a slim percentage was encouraging enough to Earl and her staff, as well as her mother. But nothing could make Lindee feel better. All her life had come tumbling down around her, and she didn't know what to do.

171

CHAPTER TEN

The sharp, insistent ring of the telephone broke through to her, and she opened one eye and closed it again quickly. The clock on the bedside table had said eleven thirty. She was sure of it. If it was correct, she'd managed to sleep twelve uninterrupted hours, and as wonderful as it had been her body still demanded more. But the telephone refused to be silent.

"Hello," she answered groggily on the twelfth ring. She didn't even bother to try to conceal her sleepy state.

"Lindee, it's Earl." His voice came quick and a little too loudly. "Listen, turn on your television set. Brooks is making an announcement. I think you'll want to hear it. I'll see you later." He hung up.

Suddenly her senses were brought to life again and the calm she'd felt when she'd opened her eyes was replaced by a rising feeling of doom. All the events of the last two days washed over her again when she thought about seeing Brooks's face on the television screen. It would be the first time since they'd been together. She'd even refused to watch television last night as the announcers had presented her concession speech.

She threw her robe over her shoulders and went downstairs, turning on the set and then going into the kitchen to pour herself a cup of coffee while the television warmed up. Her hands were shaky when she poured the hot liquid, and she told herself to be calm. Seeing him on the screen was something she'd have to do sometime, and it might as well be now.

Yesterday Lindee knew she'd let the demons overtake her, demons of her own creation, rising up out of the guilt she felt for what she'd brought on everyone around her. She'd longed for a punishment to be handed out to her, one in which she could suffer and then be forgiven. She'd thought she needed a way to feel good about herself again. She'd been as low as she could be, even wishing at times that the ground would open up and swallow her. But there'd been nothing that easy, that swift, that final. Yet what she had found was even more profound. Her friends had gathered around her with a dedication that she'd never imagined she'd find; a fierce loyalty encircled her as they awaited the election outcome together in her little house, and all the while every single one of them knew what was coming. Strangely enough, when it did her friends began making immediate plans for the next election, never referring to why she'd lost, only to the small number of votes that had made the difference. Never had she felt such an outpouring of love from a group of people.

Now she heard Brooks's voice, and she gripped her cup with both hands and walked slowly back into the living room. It wasn't until she sat down on the couch and looked at his face on the screen for the first time that she realized she was crying. The tears fell insistently, ignoring her determined resistance.

". . . while the photographer insists that he was hired in the name of Ted Bullock he admits that he never actually saw Mr. Bullock. However, he has told the local authorities that he is willing to take a lie detector test to prove that he is telling the truth. The photographer claims that he has been set up to take the blame, but he claims he can identify the man who hired him as one of Mr. Bullock's aides. Our investigation has revealed that the photographer has identified a photograph of Mr. Bullock's top aide, Glenn Riddell, as the man who approached him and paid him to follow Miss Bradley."

Brooks looked terrible. His eyes were bloodshot with dark circles under them that said he hadn't slept in a long, long while. The gauntness of his face was even further proof that he'd been busy. Although he had a suit on, it was slightly wrinkled, making him look less than prepared to go on television. While she watched him Lindee tried to tell herself there was no sympathy left in her heart for Brooks; no sympathy at all.

". . . our investigation has uncovered the payment for the film developing, purchase of the infrared lens for the camera, and detailed records of the photographer's reports to Mr. Riddell, Mr. Bullock's top aide. Mr. Bullock has issued a 'no comment' statement, but there is little doubt that before this issue is cleared, Ted Bullock will be ultimately held responsible. It is this reporter's opinion—though not necessarily the opinion of this station or its management—that Mr. Bullock has brought about a cruel injustice to Miss Bradley, to this state, and all its people."

Despite her tumultuous sense of loss at seeing the man she'd loved, she couldn't help but admit her admiration for his presentation. Cool, direct, forceful, and challenging, all at the same time.

". . . once again I am reminded of the age-old, often debated question that an incident such as this brings to mind: How much of a public person's life should be laid bare for us, and how much privacy does a public person have a right to expect? Have we made up our minds as citizens of this land that there are going to be two separate conditions, one for the private citizen and one for the public one? And really, haven't we already done that? And isn't that one of the most cited reasons for why we're losing more and more good people from the political arena? Aren't they shying away from it because of what we citizens are demanding, not in accomplishments, but in outright nosy private information? I'm reminded of our forefathers who created our Constitution and then, not satisfied entirely, added a bill of rights to assure each and every one of us to the right of privacy and other personal rights. Nowhere did any of them say in those bills that there should be a separate one for the general citizenry and

174

another for those running for office." He lowered his voice dramatically. "It's my guess that if each of you studied your own opinions, thought about your own private lives, you'd come to agree with me. There must be a separation between what the public needs to know and what an individual has the right to retain. If not, none of us has the right, do we? This is Brooks Griffin with WBCX. News follows at five."

She turned off the television when his picture faded. Her mind filled with a jumbled haze of emotions, and for a second she imagined she wasn't much better off than she had been the day before. Here she was again, crying like a child, torn between wanting to hate him and wanting to hold him, trying to figure out how she could put her life back together again. Alone.

Wanting to believe that his editorial comments had been aimed at vindicating her—certainly they were out of character for a reporter, who by definition is not supposed to comment on the news he reports—she was touched. But the cruel side of her insisted that he was merely preparing to vindicate himself should he be discovered as the mystery man whose identity had piqued the curiosity of the reporters and the public. Brooks must know that there would be many people trying to figure out who he was.

The telephone started up again, jarring her spine with its shrill ring. She knew it would be another reporter, and so she let it ring. She didn't know what she wanted to do today, the first time in so long that she didn't have an itinerary planned for her, but she'd already made up her mind she wasn't talking to another reporter.

She went upstairs to take a shower, thinking all along of how fantastic the events of the last forty-eight hours had been. She couldn't help but shake her head when she thought of how Brooks had been so cunning. He'd ruined the credibility of two politicians, he'd been able to destroy all the newfound feelings of love and security she'd found, and he'd set himself up on the path to becoming famous, all in one fell swoop. *Maybe years from now,* she thought, *I can admire it, but not now. It hurts too damned much.*

She opened her bedroom door, catching a glimpse of her mirrored reflection as she did so. In a sort of stop and go slow motion she paced toward the mirror.

If she'd thought Brooks looked bad she hadn't seen herself. Standing before the dresser she saw a face that looked years older, tragic in its sadness, full of defeat. A gasp escaped her lips. She could only hope she hadn't looked this way last night when all her friends had been with her.

Turning away would be too easy, and so she peered into the mirror for the longest time, taking in every fresh stress line, the swollen puffiness around the eyes, the red streaks drawn from her pupils, the sagging of her shoulders. She didn't let anything escape her observation.

And suddenly she lifted her chin and straightened her shoulders. She was a strong woman. She always had been, and she vowed she'd not let any man defeat her like this, nor would she let herself. What she'd done was past history, and if her friends and loved ones were willing to forgive her, then she should be willing to forgive herself. She'd lost the election. She'd paid the bitter price.

There was only one thing left that she couldn't deal with, and that was having loved Brooks with all her heart and suffering his betrayal. But somehow she'd find the courage to go on. She had to. This forlorn creature looking back at her in the mirror was not Lindee Bradley.

She took her hairbrush up and began brushing her hair with swift hard strokes over and over and over again. It was time to lift herself up from this despair she felt and get on with her life. It wasn't going to be easy, but she had to do something.

Flinging the brush onto the bed, she raced into the shower and turned on the water. She was ready to devote the afternoon to making that creature she'd seen in the mirror look more like the real Lindee Bradley.

She made up her mind with a stubborn pledge that wouldn't be denied, though she might suffer for a long time. She knew she would. It wouldn't be easy getting over Brooks. But nobody else had to know it. The world didn't have to see it. In a frenzy she began searching her closet for a pale pink silk kimono her mother had given her and insisted she save for a special occasion. This was the time, she told herself as she thumbed through her clothes.

This was the day to bring back the old Lindee Bradley, she decided. Maybe not on the inside. She still felt the throbbing pain inside her, and she told herself it would be there for a long while. But she had her pride.

After putting on her makeup she told herself she looked much better than before. There was no doubt of that. But when she looked closely she could see that there was still a trace of puffiness under her skin, and the gleam in her eyes was gone. She'd done her best, though, and all things considered she looked significantly better than she had earlier in the day.

Piling her hair on top of her head and securing it with a rubber band, she pulled out new lingerie and put it on. Then she got out her silk kimono and sprayed herself with perfume before she went downstairs, realizing she hadn't eaten since the night before.

The telephone rang once again while she made herself a cheese omelet, but she ignored it. If Earl or her mother wanted her, they could come over. Anyone else could call back tomorrow or next week.

She took her food out into an enclosed sunporch filled with green plants and white wicker, her favorite room in the house. She sat in a chaise longue and ate, enjoying the solitude and the way the sun was cutting into the room, warming her. It was a pleasant way to spend the afternoon. She thought she might just sleep there.

Later, after she'd put up her dirty dishes, she went back toward the sunroom, but the buzzing of the doorbell distracted her and she went to answer it. Pulling the thin silk robe up around her she peeked out through the glass but she couldn't see who it was. Against her better judgment she opened it, anxious to be rid of the caller who'd never taken his hand off the bell.

"Yes?" she demanded as she opened the door with a flourish.

"Lindee, I . . ."

Brooks stood there, looking even worse than he had on television, his face pale and drawn, his eyes bloodshot, dark whiskers giving him almost a sinister appearance.

An eerie sensation came over her, starting up her legs until they were shaking, then climbing up until it came to rest in the center of her being. She felt faint and her mind refused to function.

Their eyes met.

"I'm not seeing any reporters today." She grabbed the door with both hands and reached to swing it closed.

"I'm not here as a reporter," he said, thrusting his foot forward into the door and pushing against it with his shoulder.

"Look, this door can't stand a test of brute strength. It wasn't made for that," she said, and where her sense of humor came from she'd never know, because she had no idea what she was doing. Her instincts had taken over.

"Okay, say you'll let me come in and talk to you and I'll let go of the door."

"I don't want to talk to you."

"Okay, I'll do all the talking and you can just listen." He lifted up the corners of his mouth at a grim attempt at a smile.

"I don't want to hear anything you have to say."

He reached out and put his hand on hers. "I understand that, Lindee, but you've got to listen to me."

Responding as though she'd been burned Lindee yanked her hand away from his, losing her grip on the door. "Please," she said softly, moving to block his entrance. "Haven't you done enough? Leave me alone, Brooks. Get out of my life."

His eyes never left hers, and when he saw the tears well up, he said, "If you want to save this door, let me in. I'm not leaving. I'll break it down first. I've got nothing to lose."

Unwilling to give up without a fight, she pushed her hand against his chest. "No," she protested. "You've got that wrong, Brooks. I'm the one who's got nothing to lose. Now leave me alone or I'll call the police." Her voice rose. "Think of the publicity. I can take it, Brooks, but you can't."

He winced at her words and pushed against the door with one hard shove and was in. With a voice strangely twisted with dark determination he said flatly, "I'll have my say, Lindee, and then you can call the police."

Trying to regain her composure, she replied, "All right, you talk if you want to, but I don't have to listen. Frankly, Brooks, I can't imagine anything you could say that I'd be interested in hearing."

She walked through the living room and back into the sunroom and stretched out on her chaise longue, mindfully keeping her robe wrapped across her legs. Her body was on fire with the nervous impulses she was feeling.

He followed her and stood there for a long time looking at her. "Lindee, I knew you'd feel this way. I've tried to get here as quickly as I could, but if you saw me on television this morning you know why I couldn't."

She let out a high screech of a laugh that sounded closer to hysteria than anything else. "Oh, come on, don't try to tell me anything like that. Why didn't you call if you were concerned about how I'd feel?"

"Would you have talked to me?" he interrupted gruffly. "Don't bother to answer that."

"Surely you don't think you can shove your way in here and start telling me some story that's going to convince me that you're anything but the despicable monster that you are." She couldn't bear looking at him any longer. Too much torment was involved. She ran her finger along the palm of her hand, hoping she could think of something that would make him leave.

"I can't even think right now, Lindee. I'm just reacting. I haven't slept in two nights. I'm losing my job as well as the woman I love, and I've caused you so much pain I can't bear to think about it." He bent down next to her, fighting the urge to take her into his arms and kiss away all her resistance.

Her eyes widened. "Pain?" she asked incredulously. "You

179

think you know something about my pain?" Her mind raged against him. "How dare you? How dare you come in here with your pity! I don't need it. Understand?" Her voice shook and a sob welled in her throat as she jumped up from where she was sitting.

A lesser man would have left her then, Brooks thought, unable to bear witness to the agony that she bore. He reached out for her but she'd been too swift and all he got for his troubles was her sash. He held it to his lips, murmuring, "That's not it at all, Lindee, and I'm not leaving until you listen to what I have to say." He looked mournfully into her eyes. "If it's pity you think I'm feeling then it's for the two of us. We're special people, you and I, and what's happened between us must be rectified." He watched as she wrapped the loose robe around her body, and the purposeful way she did it made him want more than ever to reach out and bring her into his arms.

"Give me my sash," she demanded, and tied it in a knot around her waist when he complied. She was so near tears again she didn't trust herself to speak. All the fight was going out of her. She didn't have the mental or the physical strength to keep up this debilitating game. "Talk, go ahead. Then leave."

"Okay," he said.

They both sat down, warily glancing at each other as he leaned back on the abandoned chaise and she sat in a high-backed rocker across the room.

"Okay," he repeated with a sigh. "The morning I left you I . . ." He stopped. "I can't talk with you that far away. Move your chair over here."

She merely stared uneasily at him.

"Okay, I'll move this to where you are." He got up and started to pick up the long chaise longue.

"Wait, wait a minute." She held up her hand. The chaise was old, an antique she'd found in her grandfather's barn a long time ago. Brooks could tear it up moving it around like that and so she stood.

"Here, I'll help you," he said as he extended his hand to help her move her chair. He didn't move, knowing he must go easy with this strong-willed, fragile woman who'd given him her love and now believed he'd only used it.

"I can do it by myself, thank you." She lifted the chair and moved it over closer to the chaise, her robe separating to reveal her statuesque legs.

He began to talk slowly, taking his time. He knew that he couldn't rush her. He had to go slowly. He didn't want her to know just yet how frightened he was that he'd lost her forever. This was his last chance, if he still had any chance at all. "That's better." He sat on the nearest edge of the chaise, as close to her as he could get. "Now, the morning I left you I explained to you why I was leaving and where I was going."

"Oh, you sure did," she said haughtily. "You told me just what you wanted me to hear."

He made a face. "I'll let that pass. Mike and I made it into Houston by nine o'clock that morning. My station manager told me that Bullock had notified them of an important announcement he'd be making from the Rice Hotel at ten. I still didn't know anything."

"You mean you still didn't know if your scheme would work or not?"

He reached up and brushed his fingers through his hair in frustration, a habit that she'd come to recognize and love. Lindee cautioned herself against her thoughts.

"No, Lindee, that's not what I mean at all. Now damn it, quit interrupting or I'll never finish and you won't be able to get me out of here." He went determinedly on. "I heard about this along with all the other reporters. I couldn't believe my ears. And when I saw the pictures . . . all I could do was wait for the other shoe to fall, for Bullock to accuse me of being with you."

"If that's so, I'll bet you were terribly relieved when he kept quiet, huh?" She couldn't help the spiteful words from rushing out.

"Boy, you're a real hellion when you're mad, aren't you?" His voice was more relaxed now. Somehow he knew he was getting to her even as she lashed out at him. That knowledge filled him with a new courage and lightened his tongue. *Just don't frighten her off,* he told himself. *One step at a time.* But his heart still pounded with a rock-hard intensity. "No," he went on. "I wasn't particularly relieved. Surprised is more like it. I couldn't believe any of it. I was stunned."

She decided to stop her needless interruptions. He was quite determined to have his say, and there was no point in kidding herself—she wanted desperately to hear what he'd say. Being here with him only reinforced her awareness of how profoundly difficult the future was going to be without him.

He went on. ". . . and as soon as I had a good chance to really look at the pictures I realized the photographer only caught my back. So I raced back to the studio and talked to my boss. I told him then that I was the mystery man."

"And then he said, 'Oh good, we'll have a mystery man contest and see if the viewers can identify you.' "

They both laughed at her silly remark, a soft, self-conscious burst of spontaneity. Brooks looked over at her, searching her eyes for some sign of softening toward him. He desperately wanted to feel those same magical vibrations he'd picked up from her before.

She returned his stare in a state of utter confusion as her emotions railed against her. The awesome pain she'd come to know was fading, still ready to be easily revived, but ebbing away from her consciousness even as he was filling it. She'd heard his every word, paid the most exclusive attention to what he was saying, to every nuance.

"No, what he told me was that he wouldn't allow me to go on camera and give out that information. He called in one of the junior newsmen and told him to be ready to go on. Then he called in the station's lawyer and the chairman of the board to tell me that my contract would be irrevocably broken if I revealed my identity. That's why you didn't see me on television last night."

"I didn't watch television last night, Brooks. I was much too busy losing this election."

He reached out and tried to take her hand in his but she moved away. Instead he took the edge of her long sash and distractedly began running his fingers along it just as he'd done earlier. "My God, Lindee, if you only knew how badly I feel about that!" His voice was raw with emotion now. "I'll never be able to make it up to you, I know, but I intend to try." He reached up again and brushed her fingertips with his. "I love you, Lindee."

She pulled her hand away. "Don't start that, Brooks, or I'll ask you to leave. I thought you came to tell me about Bullock's part in this and your innocence." She tried to marshal a strong, forceful tone of voice. She intended to give him no sign whatsoever that she might be weakening.

"I said I had some things to tell you. I didn't define the categories, and you know it. Why else did you think I'd come if I didn't want to tell you how much I love you? This has got to be cleared up between us, Lindee." He took his tie in his hands and loosened the knot. "Why don't you offer me a drink? This isn't easy, you know."

Her eyes held her pain. "Creativity never is." She went into the kitchen and poured each of them a glass of cool iced tea, but when she returned Lindee saw that he'd moved to one side of the wicker sofa.

"Here," he motioned, urging her to join him on the sofa.

She put the tea down on the wicker coffee table between them and returned to her rocker.

"I'm not making any of this up, Lindee. Every word is the truth. I'll swear it, and I have witnesses if you'll let me finish." He took a sip of tea. "Now sit over here by me. This is a long story and I'm tired of talking across the room to you."

She didn't try to tell him that they'd been close enough. It wouldn't do any good. She merely got up and moved to the couch. Right now it was vitally important that he finish and leave. Her mind raced ahead of her, dreading his leavetaking, wishing there was some way she could accept this man's word.

Each second he remained here she felt her resolve slipping steadfastly away and there was nothing she could do about it.

"Okay, where was I?" He glanced over at the way she was sitting so primly near the edge of the sofa. He made sure he kept his distance. "I'm the one who did all the investigative work. Mike helped me, and we went all over Houston following leads on the photographer. We even drove back to the hill country. Finally we found a contact and traced him. Then he told us everything. He had nothing to lose. He'd already gotten his payment. But when I brought the information back into the station they wouldn't allow me to reveal my identity, my part in it. For the sake of the station, they said. And when I got ready to go on with my bulletin this morning I'd just left a meeting with all of them again in which they threatened to refuse me the right even to give out the investigative information I'd put together if I didn't cooperate with them. I thought it better to go on television and expose Bullock than to do nothing."

He couldn't read her expression. He didn't know if she was believing anything he was saying or not. But he couldn't give up now. "I'm begging for your understanding, Lindee. I love you. I feel exactly as I did the other night, only now I have the added burdens of your distrust and the shame of knowing what I did to you. It's taken every bit of bravado I've got to come here and face you, because the moment I saw your face in that picture I knew what you'd be thinking. I knew you'd hate me."

"Oh, yes, Brooks," she retorted in a choked voice. "Indeed. You pushed your way into my life and made me love you like I've never loved anyone before. Then you set me up. I'll bet you even have a national network contract in your briefcase right now." All her rage and bitterness came out, leaving her feeling weak and empty.

"That's exactly what I figured you'd think, Lindee." He stood up and began pacing the room, his voice rising with his own impotent anger. "And you know how I knew? Do you want to know how?" He didn't hesitate. "Because I knew from the beginning that you couldn't love me as much as I loved you. I knew

184

there was a question of trust between us that you wouldn't allow us to resolve. You've missed something along the way, Lindee, and I don't know how to give it to you. In many ways I guess I'm the wrong man for you, but I can't help myself. I was taught that love meant everything between a man and a woman. I had hoped against hope that when this news broke you'd keep the faith we established between us that night. But I knew you wouldn't. You don't love me like I love you."

She began to cry again. As much as she hated herself for it, she couldn't stanch the flow of tears that started, any more than she could help feeling the way she did right now. She wanted to believe him more than anything. She'd never known the power that love could hold over her, and all she could think about was how empty her life would be without him.

"I'm willing to break my contract, Lindee. I don't have one with a national network and I don't care at this point if I get one or not. I've come because I want you and I'll do anything to get you back. I did what I had to do to get my story out this morning, but if you want me to I'm willing to go back to Houston and on the five o'clock news I'll tell the entire truth. I'll talk until they cut me off, break my contract, anything. I'm willing to give it all up. Your love means more to me than anything else in the world. I don't know how else to prove it." He walked slowly over to her and stood at her side, watching the way the tears fell across her cheeks, his mind desperate with fear that she'd kick him out of her life forever.

They remained there for a long time and the only sound was of her crying. Memories flooded both their minds, each of them unwilling to move, afraid of breaking the limbo that held them there. Both of them realized the enormity of Lindee's next response. The balance swung in her hand like the pendulum of a clock, and whatever she did or said would determine their future, whether it be together or apart.

Just when Brooks thought he couldn't stand the suspense any longer she spoke, and her voice was like a beautiful song to his ears. She stood up and he held out his arms, unwilling to hold himself back another moment.

She looked up at him and her eyes were tired, but clear. She'd made up her mind. "I'm refusing your offer, Brooks. There's no need for you to go to your bosses with your demands."

He stood there and he knew he looked like a fool with his arms outstretched beckoning to her, but he couldn't give up now. Her words could be interpreted to mean anything and so he waited, his chest tight with unresolved tension.

"What's the point of having two lives destroyed? They've done it to me, and they'd love to do it to you."

He let his mind play with the way she said the word "they." Maybe, just maybe . . . "I came here because of you, Lindee. It's your life I'm worried about. I want to marry you. I told you that once before. But first I've got to have your trust, your faith, or it's no good." He swallowed hard. "What about your life?"

"I'm going to rebuild my life. I'll be just fine."

"Yes, but—"

"I just told you," she interrupted him, stepping into his open arms. "I'm going to rebuild my life . . . with you, Brooks. And I'm going to let you spend the rest of our days together showing me how important faith and trust are to us."

He put his hands on her shoulders, recognizing for the first time that she was shaking as much as he was, and then he kissed her firmly and fully as if to say that this was it. If she pulled away now she'd be telling him one thing, but if she responded that would be her final answer.

Feeling this, she inclined her head toward him and brought her arms around his neck, holding onto him with all her might. She never wanted to let him go again.

They held each other then without talking, each one taking comfort in the warmth of the moment, grateful to be together again.

Her lips clung softly to his, then she pressed her body even nearer, wanting to absorb the essence of this man she loved so deeply, and she felt him shudder as he ran a hand down her finely curved back and over her hip. She wanted to hold him to her always, and because their rediscovery was so fresh she couldn't bear to let go of him. She didn't want it to end. With one kiss he'd washed away all the despair she'd felt and replaced it with a vibrant, flowing sensation of power so overwhelming that she wanted to hold onto it forever.

But he pulled away. "Marry me?"

"Of course," she murmured, bringing her lips to his throat and kissing him.

"Now? Today? Tomorrow?"

"Of course," she replied softly. "And I'll tell it to the world. Then I'll tell them that they can keep their political games all to themselves." Love was all that really mattered to her now. Her love for this man who held her as if she might break, and his love for her.

"Are you kidding?" he answered, stepping back and taking her chin in his firm grip, lifting her face to his. "You can't be serious, Lindee. Who do you think can keep Bullock faithful to the women's rights bill now? You can't give up anything. You've got too much to offer."

Playfully she closed her eyes. "Kiss me and I'll think about it."

"Lindee, don't tease about something this important. One more time, my love. All you need is one more time. Everybody agrees you'll do it the next time. This stuff will all blow over and leave only one problem. We'll have to do quite a media blitz to reintroduce you as Lindee Bradley Griffin." Eagerly he watched her face. "I don't know how that sounds to you, but it sounds to me like the next freshman senator in Texas."

She reached out for him and brought her lips hungrily to his, answering all his questions with her caress. Her kiss moved coaxingly along his lips, and he responded in kind. She felt his body press against hers and her head began to swim as the excitement of their being together clouded her brain. "I love you, Brooks, with all my heart," she whispered, keeping her lips close to his.

"And I love you, Lindee," he answered before kissing her eyes and her forehead, her nose and the curve of her ears. "I promise you that I will always be a faithful, devoted husband. I'm declaring here and now that I'll never stop loving you, and I'll never let anything come between us again. Whatever comes up, our careers, anything." He searched for the right words. "I pledge to you that I'll never stop loving you. Nothing can stop us if we share that love together."

He kissed her then, starting at the curve of her throat, working slowly upward until he reached her lips. "Have you any idea how much I love you?" he asked.

"Mmm, I think so." She ran her fingers along the line of his jaw, telling herself she had all the time in the world to learn every line, every nuance of this man she loved so.

"Well, I intend to show you. I intend to take a lifetime to show you."

His voice became serious and she paid special attention to what he was saying, all the time thinking about how close they were in mind and in spirit.

"Lindee, I have to say something." He brushed his lips across hers. "We need to put our past behind us, all the pain, the distrust, the tragedy of our experience, and the only way I know that we can put it all in perspective is by going to your mother and Earl and apologizing. They're the only unfinished business that I know of."

She watched his eyes as he talked. "I love you for that," she smiled. "I truly do."

He kissed her on the nose. "I want to do it."

"We can go through the formality of it if you want, but I've already taken care of it. You may not believe me, Brooks, but they didn't take it nearly as hard as I'd expected."

"That's good news." He ran a finger along her throat. "God, Lindee, I don't know how else to prove to you how much I love you."

"I do," she said softly.

Moving slowly away from him, she turned and walked out of the room back to the front door. He followed her then.

"What are you doing?" he asked.

She said nothing but locked the front door with a swift twist of her wrist. She turned back and looked at him for a long time before she deliberately reached down and began to untie the knotted sash of her kimono. When she was finished she dropped the sash to the floor and started toward the staircase, unmindful of the way the silk robe parted as she walked. When she reached the first step she glanced back at him and smiled suggestively, then she let the soft fabric fall, first from one shoulder and then the other, as she walked unhurriedly up the stairway to her bedroom. With each step she took the robe edged slowly away from her body until she reached the top landing and let it fall away. She stood there for a while letting him look at her and then she turned and walked out of sight.

The sight of her like that stirred his already fired emotions to a new intensity and he shuddered as desire swept over him again and again. He longed to crush her to him; he had visions of what was about to take place, but he told himself to follow her lead. At last he'd found the woman he'd been looking for, and he wanted to know all there was to know of her. He followed her up the stairs in measured steps, confident that he was stepping upward toward his future.

She stood in the doorway beckoning him to her, but he could only stare. The sight before him was the most provocative he'd ever seen. She reached up to take down her hair and he could see the fine line of tender pale flesh in shadow.

"Wait, don't do that. Let me," he said in a hoarse whisper.

And then he was standing next to her, his fingers trembling as they freed her hair from its band and let it gently fall in chestnut waves around her face, cascading down along the gentle slope of her shoulders. Brooks pressed his face against the thick mass of hair, catching it up between his fingers and breathing in the fresh scent that filled his senses.

Tenderly he kissed her ear and smiled down at her, his dark

eyes probing her very soul. "Any more doubts, Lindee? Do you have any questions left to be answered? Tell me now."

Slowly and deliberately she shook her head from side to side. Then she brought her hands up to cup his face between them. "I have no doubts this time." She brushed her lips across his and looked up briefly to see the longing in his eyes.

"None?" he asked.

"None."

No longer in need of words, they faced one another, seeing in each other's eyes the very essence of love, feeling the glow of relief and joy as they silently vowed they were bound together for eternity. Desire flowed through them and they smiled tenderly at one another. There was a lifetime to be shared.

He took her in his arms, pulling her to him with a renewed intensity, and she opened her mouth to meet his, their souls fusing, solidifying into one.

LOOK FOR NEXT MONTH'S
CANDLELIGHT ECSTASY ROMANCES ®

Candlelight
Ecstasy Romances™

$1.95 each

At your local bookstore or use this handy coupon for ordering:

 DELL BOOKS
P.O. BOX 1000. PINE BROOK. N.J. 07058-1000

B185A

Please send me the books I have checked above I am enclosing $_____ (please add 75c per copy to cover postage and handling) Send check or money order — no cash or C.O.D.s Please allow up to 8 weeks for shipment

Name _____

Address _____ _____

City _____ State Zip _____